Jodi Taylor is the author of the bestselling Chronicles of St Mary's series, the story of a bunch of disaster-prone historians who investigate major historical events in contemporary time. Do NOT call it time travel!

Born in Bristol and educated in Gloucester (facts both cities vigorously deny), she spent many years with her head somewhere else, much to the dismay of family, teachers and employers, before finally deciding to put all that daydreaming to good use and pick up a pen. She still has no idea what she wants to do when she grows up.

A BACHELOR ESTABLISHMENT

Jodi Taylor

HEADLINE

First published in Great Britain in 2015 by
Accent Press Ltd

This edition published in paperback in Great Britain in 2019 by
HEADLINE PUBLISHING GROUP

8

Cataloguing in Publication Data is available from the British Library

ISBN 978 1 4722 6547 0

Printed and bound in Great Britain by Clays Ltd, Elcograf S.p.A.

Originally published under the pseudonym Isabella Barclay

HEADLINE PUBLISHING GROUP
An Hachette UK Company
Carmelite House
50 Victoria Embankment
London EC4Y 0DZ

www.headline.co.uk
www.hachette.co.uk

A BACHELOR
ESTABLISHMENT

Chapter One

Since no one had told her that Lord Ryde had returned to his neglected ancestral acres, Mrs Elinor Bascombe felt she was perfectly justified in feeling a little bit aggrieved when he blamed her for trying to kill him. His subsequent leap into one of his own ditches did nothing to improve *his* temper, either.

The day being blustery but fine, Mrs Bascombe, had, as usual, dispensed with the services of her groom and set out alone. Having successfully inspected the early crops in the North Field, met two of her more remote tenants and listened to their grievances without committing herself in any way, she was consequently feeling pleased with herself and life in general. She and her horse, Rufus, celebrated their brief but welcome freedom with a good gallop along Green Lane.

Spring was now considerably advanced. Soft new leaves were thrusting themselves from every shoot. Birds sang in the overgrown hedgerows and a brisk but warm breeze pushed white fluffy clouds around the sky like so many obedient sheep.

It was, Mrs Bascombe reflected, a good day on which to be alive and she intended to make the most of it. She pushed Rufus onwards and, nothing loth, he picked up the pace. The miles flew by under his easy stride, until finally, she pulled up so both horse and rider could regain their breath before turning for home.

Suspecting that the hour was later than she thought, Mrs Bascombe decided on her favourite shortcut. That this involved a brief excursion across one of Lord Ryde's fields troubled neither her nor Rufus one whit. His lordship was a careless landlord and had been absent these many years.

Mrs Bascombe put Rufus at the hedge at her usual spanking pace. He pricked his ears, shortened his stride, and cleared it with a good six inches to spare. They had only a very fleeting glimpse of his lordship, as, with a thunderous oath, he threw himself sideways, landing in the ditch with more of a squelch than a splash.

Pulling up with some difficulty, Mrs Bascombe wheeled her horse around, and more frightened than she would care to admit, returned to the scene of her crime.

'What he devil …' roared his lordship, pulling himself free from a closer inspection of his ditch than he had possibly intended that morning. Never sartorially magnificent in the first place, immersion in mud and stagnant water had not improved his appearance in any way. Coat, breeches, and boots were all liberally mired and the aroma of ditchwater hung about him.

Correctly apprehending that the unknown but furious figure before her was unhurt, and conscious that she was guilty of both trespass and careless riding, Mrs Bascombe shortened her reins prepared to flee the scene. Before she could do so, however, his lordship, hatless and stickless, strode forwards and seized her bridle. Unaccustomed to such treatment, Rufus snorted and plunged. His lordship was forced to relinquish his hold and his temper worsened.

Each contemplated the other.

Mrs Bascombe saw a tall, carelessly-dressed, hard-eyed stranger, at the moment quite pardonably flushed with rage. Some inkling began to dawn upon her.

His lordship, a stranger in his own land, had no such advantage and found himself at a loss to place her. He saw a female, well past her best years; only a little younger than he himself. Her horse, fretting to be off again, was a prime bit of blood and not at all what was proper, or indeed safe, for a female of her advanced – for a female not in her first flush of youth. On the other hand, the lady – as he reluctantly

2

must suppose her to be – was unaccompanied by a groom. He stifled his first urge, which had been to drag her from her horse and box her ears.

Now quite confident her victim was uninjured, and conscious of being very much in the wrong, Mrs Bascombe demanded to know, in haughty accents, if he was aware that he was trespassing.

The urge to physically assault her returned in force.

'*I'm* trespassing?' he exclaimed, too astonished by this barefaced gall to make a more telling retort.

'Yes, you are. I thought we had established that. This land belongs to Lord Ryde and you should be grateful his lordship has not set foot here these last twenty years, or you would find yourself up before the magistrates.'

'I am very well aware of who owns this land, madam. The question is, are you?'

A nasty, cold certainty settled upon Mrs Bascombe.

'You're Lord Ryde, aren't you?'

'I am, madam, and as such, entitled to walk my own fields without let or hindrance. I certainly do not expect to be menaced by some hoyden barely able to control her husband's horse. I do not know who you are, madam, nor do I wish to know, but I beg leave to inform you that your behaviour …'

'Is none of your business, my lord. You yourself have said you are not my husband. I am not accountable to you for my actions. And I take leave to inform you that this path has been so heavily used over the last twenty years or so that is has practically become a right of way. And that if you cut your hedges occasionally we would easily have seen each other. And that neglect of your ditches has contributed far more towards the currently – informal – state of your clothing than anything I may have done. In short, my lord, you are justly served for your neglect.'

This was too much. His lordship, wet and simmering, took a hasty step towards her, again reaching for her bridle.

3

'By God, madam, if you were mine I would beat you.'

Mrs Bascombe's mud-freckled face grew very white and still. A certain contempt showed in her eyes. Over the years, Lord Ryde had endured many women looking at him in many ways, but very few with such scathing scorn and – yes – repulsion. He was suddenly aware that she was alone, miles from anywhere, and not a soul within earshot should he decide to carry out his threat. He was conscious of a sudden shame and a need to make reparation for ungentlemanly conduct.

Too late.

She pulled herself up in her saddle.

'You are right, sir. The fault is mine. I am trespassing. My badly-managed horse and I will depart forthwith. May I suggest your time here would be better spent attempting to bring your lands into some sort of order, rather than recklessly hurling yourself under the hooves of chance-met neighbours. Good day to you.'

And then she was gone, thundering across the field and popping her horse neatly over the hedge at the far end.

His lordship, reflecting that there was nothing more irritating than being denied the last word, particularly when one was in the right, declined to re-enter his infamous ditch to retrieve his hat and stick, and stamped off back to his ancestral pile in no good mood.

Which was not improved any upon his arrival. Entering through his own front door – left ajar for some reason – he found his secretary and general factotum, Mr Charles Martin, crossing the hall. Waiting in vain for the appearance of that erratic retainer, Munch, to divest him of his coat, his lordship, in exasperation, flung it across the dusty table just inside the door.

'Good God,' said Mr Martin, surveying his employer and friend of many years in astonishment. 'What in the world has happened?'

Lord Ryde looked down at himself.

4

'I've been in a ditch, Charles. Ridden down by a madwoman. Have you ever actually seen a horse from underneath? My life flashed before my eyes. Even including those two days in Prague we agreed to forget. '

The aged retainer, Munch, put in a belated appearance, causing his lordship to reflect, as he often did, on the disadvantages of a bachelor establishment. However, since the only unacceptable alternative was to fill the place with even more unacceptable females, he was prepared to tolerate these disadvantages with good grace. Munch, however, although aged, bent, stubborn and, when it suited him, deaf, apparently had no difficulty identifying the culprit.

'Chestnut. White blaze. Blue riding habit. Rides like the devil.'

'Yes,' said his lordship, disentangling this without difficulty.

'Mrs Bascombe,' announced Munch.

Startled, his lordship looked around. 'Where?'

Munch sighed. 'Mrs Bascombe, my lord. Her land borders yours to the west.'

Enlightenment dawned. 'Ned Bascombe's wife? What the devil is he doing letting his wife career round the countryside like that?'

'Not a lot, my lord. He's dead.'

'What? Ned Bascombe's dead? Why does no one ever tell me anything?' demanded his lordship, unconsciously echoing Mrs Bascombe's complaint on her return to her own house.

'Dead these last five years and more, my lord.'

'Oh? Did she trample him into the ground, too?'

Mr Martin intervened.

'He broke his neck, I believe. Hunting accident.'

'Why don't I know this?'

'Because, sir, you never pay any attention either to your estate, or your neighbours. Because your stated intention was to arrive, raise as much money as possible, in as short a time

5

as possible, and be gone again before having to waste any time being polite to the natives.'

'Did I say that?'

'That was the abridged version, my lord. The original was a great deal more vigorously expressed.'

'Well, why should I bother? They don't care for me any more than I care for them. They can go to the devil for all I care. Mrs Bascombe first.'

The front door bell rattled. Its pealing days were long gone.

Somewhat startled, Lord Ryde and Mr Martin watched the elderly Munch embark on what his lordship privately thought of as his death-shuffle, returning moments later to announce, 'Sir William Elliot, my lord.'

Mrs Bascombe, meanwhile, had returned to her own home, Westfield, by the more conventional route, but still at her normal, headlong pace. Her particular friends, Miss Laura Fairburn and Lady Elliott had long since ceased to remonstrate with her. Her ladyship had once, long ago, mentioned her concerns to her husband, Sir William.

'Why?' she wailed. 'Why must she career all over the countryside in that fashion? It's not only unseemly, Sir William, it's downright dangerous. My dear, you must speak to her.'

This however, Sir William had refused to do and if he had his own ideas about why Mrs Bascombe felt compelled to hurtle headlong around the place on a horse more suited to a young blood than a middle-aged lady, he kept them to himself.

Westfield was an old building, modernised by Mrs Bascombe's late father-in-law. South facing, it was built of a warm, grey stone that had mellowed well. The grounds were small, and mostly turned over the production of fruit and vegetables. Like Mrs Bascombe herself, everything was neat and in its place.

Cantering up the avenue at Westfield, her front door was opened by the immaculate Porlock, her butler of many years standing, and on more than one occasion in the past, a loyal friend.

Once inside, she stripped off her gloves and glanced around in approval. Her house was clean and comfortable – unmistakeably a woman's house. No fishing rods or muddy boots littered her spotless floor. The tiles shone, the wooden furniture gleamed, and everything smelled faintly of beeswax and lemon. Crossing the hall towards the stairs, she enquired of the whereabouts of Miss Fairburn.

'Gone to visit the Misses Crosby, madam,' he replied, deftly taking her hat, gloves and whip. 'You will not have forgotten Lady Elliott is lunching with you today?'

'No. I've plenty of time to change, but thank you.'

With these words, she caught up her habit and ran lightly up to her room where her maid, Tiller, awaited her. Watching his mistress go, Porlock reflected that she had not lost as much of her youthful spring as she sometimes thought she had. Sighing, he returned to decanting the sherry. Mrs Bascombe hated the stuff, but her ladyship was partial to a glass before lunch.

Muttering darkly, Tiller assisted her mistress into a neat morning gown of dark blue and made high at the neck, admirably becoming to her plump figure. Whilst riding, Mrs Bascombe's hair had, as usual, escaped her hairnet. Tiller redressed her soft, fair hair and proffered, without hope, a very pretty lace cap with pale blue ribbons to tie under her chin. As she knew her mistress would do, Mrs Bascombe waved it aside. Tiller knew better than to press the matter. It took all of her time and energy to persuade her mistress to wear something on her head outside the house. Within her own walls, Mrs Bascombe was steadfast in her refusal.

'Thank you, Tilly. Once again you have made a silk purse from a sow's ear.'

Her maid merely sighed and despite the stiffness of her

7

left arm, began to collect up Mrs Bascombe's discarded habit and boots. Neither lady mentioned this awkwardness and Mrs Bascombe knew better than to offer to help. Reminding her mistress again of Lady Elliott, Tiller withdrew.

Running back downstairs, Mrs Bascombe again encountered Porlock, on the watch for Lady Elliott, who was a big favourite of his, and requested a moment of his time. She led the way into her parlour, a small but sunny room, papered in the modern style, where a cheerful fire burned.

'Porlock, do I understand Lord Ryde has returned to the district?'

Porlock inclined his head. 'I believe so, madam.'

'Tell me quickly, before Lady Elliott arrives. Why does no one ever speak of him? What did he do? No one even mentions his name.'

'It all occurred before your time, madam.'

'Yes, I know, but what did he do?' Recalling that carelessly dressed figure with those hard, grey eyes, she could believe him capable of almost anything.

Porlock hesitated.

'A not-unfamiliar story, madam, but none the less regrettable for all that.'

'But what did he do that was so bad?'

He sighed.

'Master Jack – as he was then, was ...' he paused, lost in the past for a moment. 'A tall boy, he was, a real Ryde, madam, if you will excuse my saying so. Athletic. Clever. He read Classics at university, I believe.'

'But you are describing a virtuous man.'

'Oh no, madam. Not at all. He had his faults. Many of them. He was careless, restless, mischievous, and very easily bored.'

'Ah.'

'Just so, madam. It's not my place to say, of course, but I always felt the old lord made a mistake not encouraging Master Jack – Lord Ryde, I should say – to interest himself in estate management. Very autocratic, the old lord. He alone must hold the reins. I sometimes wonder if Master Jack might not have shown a little more affection for the place if … if perhaps he had been given a small manor of his own to manage for himself; if he had been entrusted with a little responsibility … but old Lord Ryde wouldn't, madam. He wouldn't let him go to London either. And when one considers Master Jack's excesses perhaps he had the right of it. Be that as it may, he kept him here, dancing attendance on him. It was bound to lead to trouble.'

'What happened?'

'Well, I never heard he turned to poaching, but other than that, madam, nearly everything. Cards, of course. For very high stakes. Cockfighting, milling, slipping out to attend prize-fights, steeplechasing, you name it. He challenged Sir Matthew Reeth – he's gone now, you didn't know him – to a curricle race on the old pike road and nearly killed them both. Rumour had it he was involved in smuggling further up the coast. Nothing was ever proved though, and it was quickly hushed up.'

'But apart from the smuggling, these are the occupations of any bored young man with too much time and no occupation.'

'Indeed, madam, but …' he hesitated.

'Tell me please, Porlock. What don't I know that everyone else does?'

'There were – incidents – with the ladies, madam.'

She as conscious of sudden, irrational disappointment.

'Village girls?'

'Oh no, madam. No one eve laid *those* charges at his door. Give Master Jack his due, he stayed with his own kind. Married ladies, madam, with conveniently complaisant husbands, if you know what I mean.'

'I do. Go on.'

'Sir Matthew Reeth, madam, had a wife. A very pretty wife. And Master Jack, handsome and bored …'

'I understand, go on.'

'Only Sir Matthew wasn't quite as complaisant as he seemed. There was a meeting.'

'A duel?'

'Indeed, madam.'

'What happened?'

'They met at Cranham Woods. Master Jack deloped. The action of a guilty man, they said. Sir Matthew – a crack shot – put a bullet in him that just missed his heart. If it wasn't for the seconds and Dr Joseph, he'd have bled to death on the spot.'

Mrs Bascombe shivered.

'It hardly bears thinking about. To delope, and then stand, waiting, for a crack shot and wronged husband to take aim … What must have gone through his head …?'

'He never budged, madam. In fact, local rumour has it that he called out to Sir Matthew to take his time. There was no haste …'

He paused for a moment, lost in old memories and then pulled his attention back to the moment.

'There was, if you will excuse the expression, madam, the devil to pay. His lordship got him out of the country. Master Jack really wasn't fit to be moved, but the magistrates had been informed, so he had no choice. It nearly killed Master Jack, but his lordship was adamant.'

'But surely, Sir Matthew was the guilty party?'

Porlock's slightly wheezy voice continued expressionlessly.

'Yes, madam. But Lady Reeth and Master Jack – well, they had been caught in a very compromising situation – vey compromising indeed, ma'am, if you understand me. Not open to any misinterpretation, you could say. So Sir Matthew was the wronged man and Master Jack was bundled off abroad.'

'And never came back?'

'And never came back, ma'am.' He moved around the

room straightening ornaments unnecessarily. 'Some eighteen months later, Sir Matthew's wife was found in a similar situation with yet another gentleman, and there were expectations that old Lord Reeth would relent and recall Master Jack, especially when Sir Matthew and his wife left the district, but he remained adamant. He wouldn't have him back. His lordship felt that Master Jack had disgraced the name of Ryde. He made him a small allowance on condition he remained out of the country.'

'It seems an excessive punishment. At the time, Lord Ryde – the present Lord Ryde – must have been a very young man.'

'That was the general feeling, ma'am. Perhaps even Master Jack expected – but it didn't happen. His old lordship was very stubborn and Master Jack hardly less so. And by then, of course …'

'Yes?'

'Well, by then Master George had left Oxford and come to live with you and Mr Bascombe and as you know, the old lord took one of his fancies to him. I'm not saying any word of blame against Master George, madam. Possibly, he was not old enough to consider what Master Jack's feelings must have been. I've often thought it was a good job for his present lordship that his estates were entailed to the male line, otherwise who knows what might have happened.'

His perambulations around the room brought him to the fireplace and he busied himself with building up the fire. Straightening, he sighed.

'And if the old lord hadn't been so fond of Master George then perhaps … well, we all remember That Night, so I won't speak of it now. Bless my soul, madam, here's Lady Elliott.'

Back at Ryde House, Sir William Elliott stretched one booted foot towards a hastily kindled and somewhat inadequate fire, shifted uncomfortably in his chair, and reflected that any establishment was always the better for having a few females around. The brandy, however, was excellent, so much could be forgiven. Lord Ryde, obviously, had decided that since this morning visitor was inevitable, the ordeal could be somewhat lessened by a good brandy. He refocused to find himself under scrutiny.

'I think I remember you, Sir William. You had that high-perch phaeton. Dark green. Whatever became of it?'

Sir William peered back down the tunnel of time and smiled into the fire. 'Smashed to pieces on the Rushford road. Along with my collar bone. Lord, I haven't thought of that in years. Between m'father scolding fit to burst and m'mother weeping as if I'd been carried in on a hurdle, which actually I had been, you never heard such a racket.'

He then remembered he was addressing Lord Ryde, whose early years had consisted almost entirely of just such rackets, cleared his throat and wished to God he'd told his wife to go to the dev – that is, that he had remembered a previous engagement as soon as she first mentioned the idea of sending her husband to pay a morning visit to Lord Ryde, and ascertain his intentions.

'And I, Sir William,' she had continued, inexorably, 'will visit dear Elinor, just to give her a gentle hint that while this man is in the neighbourhood she would be very wise to remain within her own grounds, or if she must go abroad, to take the carriage.'

Sir William, amused, privately wished his wife good luck with that particular suggestion. He had been less amused when his wife insisted he escort her own carriage that morning, as if she and every other lady had not been safely driving around the district for years. In fact, he thought to himself, happily accepting another glass of excellent brandy, you would be hard put to find a safer or more sedate neighbourhood in all of England.

A slight cough recalled him to the present. The cause of this reluctant excursion was regarding him with so much quiet understanding in his eyes that Sir William quite warmed to him. He was not sure what he had been expecting; the Devil in disguise perhaps, but what he saw was a tall, loose-limbed man, whose somewhat harsh, deeply lined features and tired eyes made him look older than his actual age. Which must be around forty-three or forty-five, thought Sir William, doing a quick calculation in his head. His hair, although still plentiful, was heavily thatched with grey. His lordship's years did not lie lightly upon him.

Recalled thus to the purpose of his mission, he enquired politely as to his lordship's immediate plans.

They were as he had hoped. Lord Ryde had no plans to remain in Rushfordshire, or even in England. The estate was simply to provide the wherewithal for his next adventure. The only difference was that this time, his lordship planned to collect his own rents before disappearing again for foreign shores.

'I don't know why I had a sudden fancy to see the place again,' he said. 'But I did.'

Sir William suspected his lordship's financial circumstances had rendered this temporary retreat to his ancient home not only desirable but necessary.

'You won't be here for long then, my lord?'

His lordship did not miss the hopeful note in his voice, smiled sardonically, and returned an evasive answer.

'Far too quiet, surely,' pursued Sir William digging himself in deeper. 'Why, I can't believe the last time we had any excitement around here. Not for years. Not since ...' he broke of suddenly as he realised where this sentence was leading him. The last excitement in this particularly quiet corner of this particularly quiet county had been the occurrences of That Night.

Lord Ryde, noting Sir William's confusion, took pity upon him.

'Actually, sir, you are mistaken. Only this morning I had occasion to leap for my life. I have to say,' he continued

13

thoughtfully, 'I had forgotten I could move that quickly. But move I did. It's a miracle you see me sitting before you this afternoon.'

Sir William, gratefully clutching at his straw, enquired how this came about and listened with growing amusement to his lordship's only slightly embellished tale.

'You laugh, Sir William, but I fancy I frightened the lady. In the heat of the moment, I informed her that if I were her husband, I would beat her. In an instant, I could see I had said something wrong. It was unintentional, but I fear the lady was alarmed.'

Sir William regarded him steadily for a moment, then put down his wine. Subtly, the atmosphere in the room changed. The genial, slightly foolish country squire disappeared and what Lord Ryde suspected was the real Sir William took his place. 'That would be Mrs Bascombe.'

Lord Ryde nodded. 'I believe so, yes.'

'That is unfortunate indeed.' He glanced sharply at his lordship. 'I wouldn't normally gossip, of course, and especially about Mrs Bascombe, a lady who has endured more than her share of misfortune, but it occurs to me that, indirectly, this particular tragedy involves your family, if not you yourself.'

His lordship put down his own glass.

'How so?'

'Mrs Bascombe ... Elinor Bascombe was old Wilmot's daughter. You remember him, I expect. All to pieces and selling off his daughters to the highest bidders. Mr Bascombe senior favoured the match. Ned was always rather wild, of course, but she had breeding and character and it was hoped, I think, that she would steady him. And I think she did, for a time. Certainly while Ned's father was alive. He was very fond of her, quite doted on her in fact. Well, all that changed after his death. Ned went to the devil just as fast as he could go – drinking, gambling, you name it. And he wasn't an amiable drunk, either, if you take my meaning.'

14

Lord Ryde silently cursed himself and nodded.

'Ned went up to London, which brought her some relief, but of course, the temptations there were much greater. Mrs Bascombe remained at home, and being a woman of intelligence, did what she could to stem the haemorrhage of money. It was useless, of course. The more she found from the estate, the more he demanded of it. In ten short years, he ran through nearly everything. I think, although I've never asked, that she and their agent, Masters – a very sound man, I'm happy to say – were able to squirrel away some small amounts out of his reach. Small enough not to be noticed. Illegal of course, but who could blame them? Ned, I'm sure, suspected something of the kind and employed every means to discover the truth. It was around this time that Mrs Bascombe suffered a number of – falls – that frequently prevented her appearing in public. I'm proud to say Lady Elliott made a point of calling at Westfield at least once a week to see her. And sometimes, I went too.'

He paused to pick up his brandy again.

Lord Ryde felt slightly ashamed of his earlier impatience with his visitor. That this apparently unexceptional, kindly, and undoubtedly overworked family man and his wife had found time, every week, to drive to Westfield ... he could imagine Sir William and Lady Elliott, quietly but firmly insisting on seeing Mrs Bascombe. And her husband reined-in only because he knew that at least once a week, he would have to present his wife ...

Sir William continued. 'Well, Ned was going to hell in a handcart and we thought things were about as bad as they could be – and then his younger brother, George Bascombe, arrived.

His lordship's attentive expression shut down. He reached for his brandy, saying languidly, 'I cannot believe the appearance of Mr George Bascombe could possibly improve any situation, far less this one.'

Sir William regarded him steadily. 'Well, you have your

own reasons for saying that, my lord. I won't deny there's good and bad in the boy – well, he's a man now, I suppose. I don't know the ins and outs, so I won't comment, if you don't mind.'

His lordship inclined his head.

'Things did get worse. Very much worse, as you know. Georgie summed up the situation at a glance and immediately appointed himself his sister-in-law's protector. There were some dreadful scenes apparently, and, I'm ashamed to say, I was several times on the point of instructing Lady Elliott to cease her visits. It seemed to me that we were heading towards a tragedy. And I was right.'

'Allow me to refill your glass.'

'Thank you. Just a little, if I may. Well, there was a frightful scene one night. You know the night I mean. Creditors besieging the house. Ned desperate for money. Any money. Obtained anyhow. He started on Elinor, of course. George was out that day, shooting, I believe. He arrived back at Westfield to find his brother shaking Mrs Bascombe by her hair and that's putting it rather mildly. Blood was running down her face. George stepped in and Ned, who was, if you remember, bigger than both of them put together, gave George the thundering good thrashing he thought he deserved.

'Georgie, to his credit, picked himself up and rattled in again, calling to Elinor to lock herself in her room. The poor girl could barely stand, however. Ned picked up George and bodily slung him out of the house. The lad had no coat, no hat, was in his shirtsleeves, in fact. He tried to get back inside, and Ned, seizing a pistol from somewhere, first threatened him and then fired at him as he ran down the avenue. He would have hit him, too, at that range, but Mrs Bascombe threw herself at him and spoiled his aim.'

'At some risk to herself, surely?' murmured Lord Ryde.

'Indeed, yes. George escaped into the darkness and Ned, blind with rage, turned his attention to the one person still

16

within his reach. She probably owes her life to Porlock and her maid, Tiller, who bravely intervened and tried to get her away. Porlock was knocked down and Tiller had her arm broken. It never mended properly. And later that night, Mrs Bascombe lost the child she'd been carrying.'

He stopped and drank his brandy.

Lord Ryde stared at him. 'Good God, this is appalling. Frightful is not the word to describe it. How did he escape the consequences?'

'Well, again as you know, my lord, George fled to your father at Ryde House and we all know what happened next. The events at Ryde House rather overshadowed those at Westfield. However, old William Crosby, who was alive then, Sir Timothy Relton, Mr Osborne from Whittington, and I all visited Ned Bascombe together and gave him to understand that such behaviour would not be tolerated in this neighbourhood. He was, I think, more than a little frightened at his actions and for two or three years we had no trouble from him. Mrs Bascombe recovered – although not completely, I suspect, and they lived reasonably peacefully until he took a bad toss out hunting one day, and was brought home dead. No great loss.'

'And after he visited Ryde House that night, Mr George Bascombe,' said Lord Ryde, carefully 'was never heard of again.'

Sir William returned the hard glare. 'Not by me, my lord. Nor anyone else that I know.'

'What of Mrs Bascombe? If she and George were so close …?'

'It was nearly twelve months before Mrs Bascombe was completely restored to health. And since then, her time – all her time – has been taken up with restoring and managing her husband's estates. Considering what she was left with, my lord, her achievement has been remarkable. The first years were hard, but she got rid of all the useless short-term tenants milking the land for every penny. It's taken a while, but she has finally pulled it all together and, I think, should Mr George Bascombe ever return, he will find himself in possession of a very snug little estate.'

His lordship spoke harshly. 'But he won't return, will he? He won't ever return. How can he after he murdered my father?'

Chapter Two

Back at Westfield, the ladies, having enjoyed a delightful luncheon, during which the conversation covered Miss Clara Elliott's impending Season, the recalcitrance of tenants in general and the occupants of Northridge Farm in particular, the correct method of removing stains from silk, and a recipe for braised ham, were each wondering how to introduce the topic uppermost in both their minds – Lord Ryde.

Eventually, a brief digression into a trifling accident by her second son, Gilbert, which had resulted in a sprained ankle, gave Lady Elliott the opportunity for which she had been waiting.

Those who stigmatised Leonora, Lady Elliott, as a plump pigeon whose only interests lay in food and family, did her a grave disservice. True, as the devoted mother of an adventurous family, she was inclined to over-anxiety, but at heart, she was a sensible woman and very much aware of the way the world worked.

'My dear,' she said, casually, as Porlock helped her to a damson tartlet. 'Oh, no, just one, I think, well, all right, possibly another, since they look so good, thank you, where was I? Yes. Elinor, my love, I have just a tiny thing to mention and I know you will not be alarmed and indeed, there is no need for you to ... although I do think that in future, just until he departs, which should be quite soon for I don't know what on earth could bring him here in the first place, but just until he does, Elinor, I do think you should, perhaps, curtail your excursions, just until – not that I wish to alarm you in any way, and let's face it, he must be forty-five if he's a day and his lifestyle cannot have been conducive to good health, can it? I mean, he can probably barely walk these days. Gout, you know, like old Sir Timothy, poor soul, and they do say that an intemperate lifestyle can disorder the intellect which must be true, because when I remember Sir William's late father ... I mean, he may not even be responsible for his actions, so you see, my love, it's best for you to remain quietly at home for the next few weeks.'

Fortunately, Lady Elliott was an old friend, and having met Lord Ryde only that morning, Mrs Bascombe was able to disentangle this with ease. Watching Porlock smilingly present her ladyship with a third tartlet, she waited until her friend had taken a bite and then casually remarked, 'Oh, if you mean Lord Ryde, I'm very sorry to have to mention this, Leonora, but I met Lord Ryde this morning, when I tried to kill him. I suspect that in future, Lord Ryde will be remaining indoors to avoid *me*. So you need have no worries at all,' she concluded brightly, conveniently forgetting the sickening feelings she had experienced as his lordship had appeared, albeit fleetingly, directly beneath her horse's hooves.

Lady Elliott choked on a stray crumb. Porlock retreated to the sideboard from where he could unobtrusively observe events.

'Well, not deliberately tried to kill him, of course,' continued Mrs Bascombe, rather too quickly. 'I took a hedge and there he was, right under Rufus's hooves. Although not for long. And you don't have to worry about gout. He seemed quite spry to me.'

Lady Elliott regarded her friend in speechless shock.

'Anyway, he pulled himself out of the ditch, cursed me soundly, and stamped off home,' said Mrs Bascombe, abbreviating the morning's events out of consideration for her friend. 'I wouldn't be at all surprised if he packed his bags and is gone again by this time tomorrow. With luck, never to return. Shall we have some tea? Oh, thank you, Porlock.'

Lady Elliott was never speechless for long.

'But my dear …? Elinor …?'

Mrs Bascombe toyed briefly with the idea of changing the subject, just to tease her friend, but relented.

'It really is all right, Leonora. His lordship and I parted on such terms as to preclude any possible future contact. And even if it were not so, how could I possibly pursue any acquaintanceship with the son of the man my husband's brother is accused of murdering?'

Lady Elliott paused to work this out and then plunged back into the conversation.

'Oh, Elinor, when I think back to That Night ...'

Mrs Bascombe's face quivered. Porlock put down his tray and waited quietly to see if he would be needed, but she recovered almost instantly.

Lady Elliott continued. 'It was all so long ago and yet still ... Will things never be resolved?'

'How can they be until George returns? And if he ever does then he's a fool. Robbery and murder? How can he ever set foot in England again?'

Silence filled the room, for this was a long-held bone of contention between them. Whilst Lady Elliott agreed that it had been Elinor's duty to remain at Westfield in the aftermath of her husband's death, she maintained on every occasion possible, that now the estate was showing a small profit, her friend could consider herself released from any obligations thereto and re-join the world.

Mrs Bascombe, whose meagre portion had long since been swallowed up in the vast maw of her husband's debts, and who now had barely a penny to her name, could not agree. To move to London, or more probably Bath, would indeed be agreeable. Bath, with its wide society and sparkling social life was very tempting to a lady who had barely stirred from this neighbourhood in nearly twenty years. No one was more conscious than Mrs Bascombe that the best years of her life were long behind her; gone beyond recall. Financial necessity had obliged her to remain at Westfield. Social convention kept here there and, as she sometimes admitted to herself in the small hours, fear prevented her leaving. These days, Westfield was a very

21

comfortable place and she was highly regarded by neighbours and friends. She sometimes wondered what would happen to her should George, or more likely, George's heir, return to claim his inheritance. Then, obliged to leave her home, her future would be bleak indeed, for Mrs Bascombe had no intention of remaining at Westfield, dependent upon the kindness of strangers. She had been her own mistress, and mistress of Westfield for too long. No, in the unlikely event of George or his heir appearing to claim their own, she would go quietly, but where to and how she would live were subjects she could not contemplate without strong misgivings. The best she could hope for was that a small cottage might be found for her somewhere on the estate, where she could live quietly with her friend, Miss Fairburn; their social circle restricted to those who cared enough to visit two ladies living precariously on the fringes of genteel poverty.

She was unaware of how much of this showed on her face. Lady Elliott reached over to take her hand and Porlock, without being asked, gently placed a small glass of wine before her.

'My dear,' said Lad Elliott softy, 'your friends will never allow that to happen.'

Mrs Bascombe nodded, somewhat blindly, because the offer was kindly meant and no one, not even Miss Fairburn, knew how unacceptable it would be to her.

The silence was broken by Porlock, softly observing that he believed Miss Fairburn had returned.

Lady Elliott stayed long enough to enquire after Miss Fairburn's health and that of her family, for, in addition to a naturally kind heart and a genuine interest, she had been bred up always to be civil to those in less fortunate circumstances than herself.

Miss Fairburn, the oldest daughter in a large and cheerful family from Oxfordshire, had long since realised her duty to her family meant stepping aside for younger and prettier sisters. She had accepted this with some sadness of spirit, but without rancour, foreseeing that her future role was that of maiden aunt. Before this hideous fate could come to pass however, she had received a letter from Mrs Bascombe, a friend of her childhood, offering her the position of companion and, should it ever be required, chaperone. Relieved of the guilt incurred by living upon the goodwill of members of her family, no matter how kindly meant, she had no hesitation in accepting a position to live at Westfield with her friend.

Mrs Bascombe was congenial company and Westfield today was both comfortable and well run. Like her friend, she too often wondered what the future would hold for her when the day came – as it surely would – when they had to leave Westfield. If Mrs Bascombe no longer required, or more likely, could not afford her services, then, she supposed, it would mean returning to her family and caring for her elderly mother and her many nieces and nephews. She occasionally wondered about becoming a paid companion to another lady, but knew in her heart that no matter how liberal the household, nor how easy-going the mistress, she would never be lucky enough to find another Westfield. She was a prudent woman, however, and her living expenses proving very small, she had put away as much as she could against the day when she and Elinor would find themselves adrift in the world.

After Lady Elliott's departure, Mrs Bascombe lost no time in acquainting Miss Fairburn with the events of the morning. Unlike Lady Elliott, however, Miss Fairburn was entrusted with the whole story. At its conclusion, she contemplated her friend, with expressions of amusement, concern, dismay, and astonishment all flitting, one after the other, across her face.

'Elinor …' she said, half laughing, half appalled. 'I leave you for one morning … was he hurt at all?'

'I don't think so,' said her friend, honestly. 'If he was, it

23

certainly didn't prevent him expressing himself with great fluency. And volume.'

'He must have been very much displeased.'

'Beautifully understated, my dear Laura. He was very much displeased. Displeased to the extent of offering me bodily harm.'

Miss Fairburn stopped smiling. 'Well, I suppose one could say he abandoned any pretensions to the title of "gentleman" some years ago. I wish I had been there.'

'My dear, by that time he practically had Rufus' hoof-prints across his chest. And on his own land, too. There is perhaps some excuse.'

Miss Fairburn would have none of it.

Perversely, Mrs Bascombe felt compelled to defend his absent lordship. 'Whilst not condoning his behaviour in any way, my own was not above reproach. And no harm was done, except perhaps to Lord Ryde's dignity. Lady Elliott has been advising me to remain within our own grounds during his visit, which we hope will be a very fleeting one. Masters is calling tomorrow and with a list of items for discussion that must be almost as long as my arm. By the time I emerge from our meeting it will be next week at least and his lordship will be gone. Which reminds me – do you know which room Mrs Stokesley has allocated Mr Masters? He will have it that it is improper to stay here, but I think, given his – and our – advancing years, no scandal could possibly be brewed, even by our own enthusiastic rumour-mongers, don't you agree?'

'Oh yes. And he a happily married man these last thirty ears. How can people gossip so?'

'In this sedate part of the world, what else is there to do? Apart from Sir William Elliott, you and I appear to be the only people here with more tasks than time.'

'How true. Mr Masters will be in the Green Room, by the way. Far enough away from the defenceless ladies, but still actually in the main body of the house as befits his trusted position. As usual, Mrs Stokesley and Porlock have it exactly right. What time does he arrive tomorrow?'

'Quite early, I believe. Certainly before eleven o'clock.'

'Oh, Elinor, what a shame. Roberts informs me the weather is set fair for at least the next three days and you'll be stuck inside.'

'Ah well, it can't be helped. And our discussions are so much more pleasant these days. Imagine – we actually discus the allocation of profits, such as they are, rather than plotting how to delude and distract our creditors. You cannot imagine how pleasant that is. So, tell me, how do the Misses Crosby do?'

Lady Elliott visited several times over the next week to share news and gossip about the newcomers over tea and cakes. Initially, hopes had been high that his lordship meant to settle at last. He had sent for his agent, an understandably depressed and dispirited man named Reynolds, and after the meeting, Reynolds had scuttled away with armfuls of papers and a harried expression. It transpired, however, in the way things mysteriously get around, that Lord Ryde was enduring the hardships of his family home only to ensure that every last possible penny possible could be wrung from his neglected estate.

'What a shame,' remarked Mrs Bascombe, helping Lady Elliott to another slice of cake. 'Although, when I … encountered … him, he was actually inspecting a ditch.'

'Looking for loose change, perhaps,' suggested Miss Fairburn, acidly.

Miss Fairburn was a tall, slender woman with dark hair and eyes and a long, clever face, and might have been formed to provide a complete contrast to her friend, the shorter, plumper, fair-haired Mrs Bascombe. This contrast manifested itself further in their natures. Miss Fairburn was never anything other than calm, collected, and quiet, while Mrs Bascombe fizzed with barely suppressed energy from morning to night. Energy denied a natural outlet has to go somewhere and Mrs Bascombe's manifested itself, as Sir William had correctly guessed, in headlong gallops around the countryside. Gallops during which, Mrs Bascombe sometimes thought, it would be no bad thing if she followed her husband's example and broke her own neck.

Sir William entertained respect and affection for his wife's friend and only the conviction that George Bascombe would never reappear and Mrs Bascombe would be allowed to live out her days in peaceful seclusion at Westfield kept him from making his concerns known to his wife.

At eleven the next morning, Mrs Bascombe awaited the arrival of her agent, Masters, a cautious and taciturn man, traditional in his values, who deplored everything modern. He bowed low, for he had an admiration for Mrs Bascombe, and she for him. Mr Masters, meeting Mrs Bascombe for the first time many years ago, found himself having to revise his previously unflattering opinion of women in business very quickly indeed, and given the condition of the estate, Mrs Bascombe's opinion of him had been no better. Each soon realised they had misjudged the other and a profitable partnership was born from that moment. She knew better than to distract him with pleasantries and after a brief enquiry as to the health of his wife and family, seated herself at the long table in the library and pulled the first of her papers towards her.

Considerably improved the estate may have been, but it seemed there were still a hundred thousand things to discuss, mull over, plan for, make provision for, veto, or set in hand. For three days they laboured, until finally, each pronounced themselves satisfied with the progress made. Gathering up his papers, Masters declined any offers of further hospitality, citing pressure of business and promised to let her have the appropriate documents for signature within seven days. They parted as amiably as ever and Mrs Bascombe, suddenly

26

found herself at liberty. For a second she hesitated; Mrs Stokesley, the housekeeper, had been petitioning for a review of the contents of the linen cupboards, but the sun was shining – who knew for how long?

Mrs Bascombe changed into her riding habit without feeling the need to trouble Tiller in any way, and using the back stairs, guiltily made her way to the stables. She was not, however, as deaf to Lady Elliott's pleas as she had appeared, and presently flew from the stable yard, admittedly at top speed, but this time accompanied by her groom, Roberts.

She had no clear intention of going as far as the sand dunes, but once there, it seemed a shame not to venture onto the sands themselves. A stiff wind blew onshore and foamy white breakers crashed onto the glistening sand. Spray flew and she could taste the salt on her lips.

Rufus snorted impatiently, for he knew what was coming next. Mrs Bascombe and her groom eyed each other for a moment and then each urged their horse forwards. Neck and neck they plunged through shallow water, racing flat out. Both horses stretched their necks and lengthened their stride, flying across the wet sand and splashing through pools of sea water. Exhilaration coursed through her veins as she felt the wind, sea, and wet sand in her face. Faster and faster, the two horses thundered across the deserted shore. A few rare minutes of freedom. Of fun.

All too soon, she was pulling up. The horses dropped to a canter, then a walk, while everyone got their breath back. Beside her, Roberts was wiping his face. Guiltily aware of what Lady Elliott would say if only she could see her now, Mrs Bascombe attempted the same with a very inadequate handkerchief. She was conscious that her hair had again escaped its restraints and her habit was liberally splattered with wet sand and foam. Her hem was sodden to a good six inches.

'I must look like a gypsy,' she said, laughing.

'Ah,' said Roberts, refusing to comment.

27

They left the beach, picking their way back through the dunes to pick up Green Lane, which would eventually lead back to her own property on the western side and Lord Ryde's to the east. Mrs Bascombe was fully occupied in restoring her appearance, tucking in her hair and brushing the worst of the sand from her habit and so did not notice the oncoming riders.

'Ah,' said Roberts, by way of directing her attention.

'Oh, da – dear,' said Mrs Bascombe. Having spent the last three days closeted with her agent, the presence of Lord Ryde had slipped her mind.

'Mm,' said Roberts, varying his conversational range.

Lord Ryde, meanwhile had also perceived that he and Mr Martin were Not Alone.

'Brace yourself, Charles,' he muttered to his companion.

Mr Martin had already made an informed guess as to the identity of the oncoming riders and permitted himself a small smile of anticipation.

Mrs Bascombe found herself at a loss. There was no doubt that however unconventional their first meeting had been, they had met. Was it more or less rude to pass by in silence? Or essay a frigid nod of acknowledgement but nothing more, indicating a disinclination to further intercourse? Or exchange polite greetings as if nothing had happened? Since she still perceived herself to be the wronged party, she was conscious of a strong feeling that nothing less than his lordship hurling himself from his horse and abasing himself on the ground at her feet would be adequate.

A slight cough from Roberts recalled her from this pleasant picture. Both gentlemen had politely pulled to the side of the lane and halted. Mrs Bascombe drew level. The gentlemen touched their hats. Mrs Bascombe inclined her head, regally. Another three strides and she should be safe. Slightly behind his lordship, Mr Martin struggled to keep a straight face. Roberts, who like all good servants knew

28

everything and said nothing, stared woodenly between his horse's ears. Mrs Bascombe met his lordship's eyes. The moment was pregnant.

'Mrs Bascombe, I presume. How do you do, ma'am?'

Mrs Bascombe was interested to note he had apparently gone to the trouble of discovering her identity. So much for any hope of remaining anonymous.

'Lord Ryde; I believe we are neighbours.'

'So I understand,' he assented gravely.

Silence fell

'May I introduce Mr Charles Martin, ma'am? Charles, this is Mrs Bascombe, of whom you heard me speak, not briefly, the other day.'

Mrs Bascombe, who had been eyeing Mr Martin with some curiosity, was unable to shake hands, but smiled warmly upon him instead. As Lord Ryde had, at their first meeting, been at a loss to place her, so did Mr Martin puzzle Mrs Bascombe. Unlike his lordship, carelessly but expensively dressed, Mr Martin's attire was quiet and modest, but his horse was good. She liked his square-set, open face, and his unruly curls. His brown eyes twinkled mischievously as he responded gravely to her greeting.

Returning her attention to his lordship, she prepared to be provocative.

'I am relieved to see you recovered, my lord. I feared after so severe an accident that you would be laid upon your bed for some time. Is it wise to be up and about so soon?'

'I thank you for your concern, madam, but I am not so aged and infirm as you apparently believe.'

'No,' she agreed, affably. 'You couldn't be.'

Mr Martin assumed an intent survey of the horizon.

'Although, had I known you were abroad, madam, I might well have thought twice before venturing forth. One cannot be too careful.'

'Not at your age, no.'

His lordship, who had once or twice considered how to

apologise for his behaviour without in any way revealing himself to be familiar with her past history, once again cast good manners and breeding to the four winds.

'May I ascribe the fact that the countryside does not appear to be littered with your victims, to your having brought your groom along to help you control your horse?'

'No, you may not,' she replied imperturbably. 'You may ascribe his presence to Lady Elliott's belated warning as to the imprudence of riding alone these days.'

'You amaze me, ma'am. I had not supposed you so timid. My understanding is that this is one of the safest neighbourhoods in the county.'

'Until last week, sir, you would have been perfectly correct. You are, however, behind the times. How sad it is when one is no longer able to keep abreast of current events.'

'Being usually at the centre of current events, ma'am, I have no need to keep abreast.'

Although he could tell that both protagonists were thoroughly enjoying themselves, Mr Martin thought it wise to intervene.

'Fine weather for the time of year, do you not agree, Mrs Bascombe?'

He was rewarded with another brilliant smile.

His lordship did not grind his teeth.

'Very pleasant,' she agreed. 'One is certainly tempted to take every opportunity to enjoy it.'

'Is that what you've been doing?' demanded Lord Ryde, surveying her still somewhat dishevelled appearance. 'One would have supposed you to have been working in a ditch.'

'As opposed to actually jumping into one?' retorted Mrs Bascombe, her own good resolutions melting like so much snow in the August sun.

'You must not allow us to keep you standing, ma'am. I know how difficult it is for you to control your horse.'

Rufus, who had been standing like a rock throughout the entire conversation, looked somewhat surprised.

Sensitive as always to comments about her horse, Mrs Bascombe stiffened and was about to utter a blistering reply when several things happened at once. Something large stirred from behind the hedge, prompting a bird to erupt noisily from the tangled greenery. The bird shot diagonally across the lane, almost under Rufus's nose, uttering a harsh call of alarm as it did so.

All the horses jumped but Rufus himself shied sideways, almost colliding with Lord Ryde's long-backed grey. Already in the act of transferring reins and whip to her other hand, and preparing to move on, Mrs Bascombe was caught unawares. A loud report very close to her ear made her jump violently and unnerved Rufus even further.

To Lord Ryde, things began to move very slowly. Gaining control of his own mount, he looked for Mrs Bascombe, half expecting Rufus to be at least three fields away by now.

Mrs Bascombe, however, was sitting perfectly still, a strained expression of shock and bewilderment on her face.

Time slowed even further.

She pressed a hand against her shoulder, took it away again, and stared in perplexity at the bright red stain across her palm.

Lord Ryde, who knew a gunshot when he heard one, was already swinging himself down from his horse. Throwing his reins to a shocked Mr Martin, he strode forwards. As he reached up to help her, her eyes refocused and all the colour swept from her face. His lordship saw she still had a smear of mud across one cheekbone. White lipped, she whispered, 'I believe I have been shot!' and fell from the saddle into his arms.

31

Chapter Three

Time started up again. Sound came back into the world. Mr Martin, momentarily paralysed with horror, watched his lordship gently lower Mrs Bascombe to the ground and rip off his cravat to attempt to staunch the flow of blood. Like his lordship Mr Martin also recognised gunfire. Cursing the fact that riding in England meant his saddle holster was empty, he stood in his stirrups, vainly attempting to peer over the tall hedges in an effort to locate the culprit.

'You,' demanded Lord Ryde of Roberts. 'Do you know where the doctor can be found?'

Roberts, a good deal astonished but not, as far as his lordship could tell, at all afraid, replied at once, 'Yes, my lord. It's not far from here.'

'Then get yourself off at once. Bring him back to Ryde House – it's nearer than Westfield. We'll get your mistress back there. After you've found the doctor, ride to Westfield and tell them what's happened. Try not to alarm them too much.'

Roberts nodded.

'Is there someone capable you can bring back to assist with the nursing?'

'Ah. Miss Fairburn, my lord. Mrs Bascombe's friend and a cool head on her.'

'Good. Off you go. Hurry, man.'

Roberts wheeled his horse around and departed with haste.

'Charles!'

'My lord?'

'Back to Ryde House. Get a cart – anything in which we

can lay her flat. Tell Munch what has happened here. Hot water. Bandages. You know the drill.'

'Yes sir.' Mr Martin paused briefly to rip off his own cravat and rummaged for a handkerchief. These he handed over and then he too was galloping away.

Lord Ryde wadded his friend's cravat into a ball and pressed it over the wound. Within seconds, it was as blood-soaked as the first. His lordship's face grew grim. With a muttered curse, he pulled a small penknife from his pocket and began to cut through Mrs Bascombe's clothing, eventually laying bare a ragged hole from which blood was still flowing.

Mrs Bascombe's eyelids fluttered and her eyes focused. She became aware of his lordship tugging at her clothing and uttered a small, distressed sound.

'Please remain still, Mrs Bascombe,' said his lordship with a calm he was far from feeling. 'You have sustained a small wound. I am endeavouring to stop the bleeding.'

She was not completely aware of her surroundings and tried again to cover herself.

'I'm sorry,' said his lordship gently, 'but I must see what I'm doing. Please close your eyes and let me work.'

To Mrs Bascombe, this seemed very sound advice. By closing her eyes, she could pretend none of this was happening. A sharp jolt of pain dispelled this happy thought. Her eyes flew open. She groaned, lifted her head, and again tried to pull her clothing across her exposed breast.

'Very well, ma'am,' said Lord Ryde. 'You may make yourself useful.' He took her hand and pressed it against the makeshift bandage. 'Press here. Hard. That's it. That's my good girl.'

He began to rummage in his own pockets, pulling out a handkerchief. His eye alighted on Mrs Bascombe's hat, lying a few feet away, her blue scarf trailing from its crown. He ripped it off, folded his handkerchief into a pad, applied that to the wound as well, and knotted the whole in place with her scarf.

Satisfied, he sat back on his heels to consider what else might be done.

Like Mr Martin, he was listening for any indication their attacker might still be in the vicinity – possibly reloading or pulling out a second pistol, but some minutes had passed now since the original shot. If their assailant had a second attack in mind, he was taking his time.

The hair on the back of his neck had risen and he was conscious of what a target he must present, but apart from his own rapid breathing, he could hear nothing and told himself it was only a careless poacher. That a poacher would hardly be out about his business at four o'clock on a sunny spring afternoon was highly improbable.

Mrs Bascombe lay quietly, eyes closed, her breathing very shallow.

His lordship said commandingly, 'Mrs Bascombe!' and her eyes flickered open again. He awaited the inevitable, 'What happened?' from a lady lying sprawled upon the ground with her clothing torn away, but even now, Mrs Bascombe departed from the norm and demanded to know, albeit faintly, if anyone else was hurt.

'Just you, ma'am. Please lie still. Your groom has gone for the doctor. Charles has departed to find a conveyance. Please keep very still and try to remain calm.'

He felt slightly foolish as he said this, for indeed, like a model patient, Mrs Bascombe was lying still and for a woman who had just been shot, she seemed remarkably calm.

He would have liked to stand up and look around these tall hedges, if only to reassure himself their attacker had taken advantage of the confusion following his shot and made good his escape, but when he looked down, Mrs Bascombe had grasped a fold of his riding coat and was holding very tightly.

Slightly touched, he smiled and put his hand over hers,

34

saying, 'Not long now, Mrs Bascombe. We'll take you back to Ryde House and then you will be comfortable again.' That no one could ever be comfortable at Ryde House was something better not mentioned at this point.

She made no response. She had again turned very pale. His lordship checked his dressing was secure, shivered in the suddenly chilly wind, and wished very much that Charles would miraculously reappear with a conveyance, although he could not have been gone more than a quarter of an hour. He could hardly have reached Ryde House yet.

However, he was mistaken. Only a few minutes later he heard and felt the unmistakeable sound of approaching hooves and the rattle of a wagon. Mr Martin appeared, accompanied by an enormous man in a full frieze coat and gaiters, driving a farm cart.

'He was just down the road,' said Mr Martin, dismounting. 'He heard the shot and was coming to investigate anyway.

Mrs Bascombe made a small sound.

'Just a minute, Charles.' He stripped off his coat and gently covered her. The driver too had climbed heavily down, took one look at Mrs Bascombe, and vigorously called for God to bless his soul.

'Quite,' said his lordship. 'Do you hold your horse while we lift her on board.'

'No need, yer honour,' said the driver brusquely. 'She'll stand quiet.'

Between the three of them, they lifted Mrs Bascombe into the cart, a proceeding she bore quietly and with no complaint, and made her as comfortable as they could. Mr Martin was despatched ahead to alert the Munches. The driver shook his reins his horse lifted her head and they moved off with the best speed they could safely muster.

The journey back to Ryde House was bumpy and Lord Ryde had much to do to keep his passenger as unjolted as possible. Several times he nearly dammed the driver's eyes

35

but recognised the farmer must get Mrs Bascombe to safety with all possible speed and held his tongue.

Lord Ryde had been too busy attending to her wound to spare a thought for any other subject, but sitting now in the back of this bouncing cart he found he finally had enough time to turn his mind to this incredible occurrence. And incredible was the only word for it. This was England. Not only that, this was, as he had frequently been assured, and knew from his own bitter experience, one of the safest and most sedate neighbourhoods in that safe and sedate country. People – ladies especially – were not publicly shot at. Not often, anyway. What on earth could Mrs Bascombe have done to incur such enmity? His lordship resolutely banished the frivolous suggestion that he might not have been her only victim. He could not help smiling a little at the thought of this neighbourhood being positively strewn with others who had fallen under Rufus' hooves, but dismissed the idea. A particularly severe bounce recalled his mind to the present emergency. He and Charles could discuss this later.

Lord Ryde had expected to follow Green Lane back to Ryde House, but the driver turned off and cut across country. He opened his mouth to protest and then closed it again. Presumably the fellow knew what he was about.

His trust was rewarded. In a surprisingly short space of time, they were trotting up the avenue and Mr Martin came hurrying down the steps to meet them.

'You go on, sir,' he said. 'I'll see to the driver and join you shortly.'

He reached into his pocket as he spoke, but the driver loudly rebuffed any attempt to reward him, saying brusquely he wanted no reward for bringing Mrs Bascombe back safe, no, nor would anyone else around here, so he could put that right back in his pocket now. Sir. He picked up his reins, cast a stern glance at Mr Martin and informed him he should get himself inside – them Munches were a feckless pair and his lordship would have need of him.

'Well, thank you anyway,' said a chastened Mr Martin.

'Ah,' he replied, displaying a possible relationship to Mrs Bascombe's Roberts, and took himself away.

Running up the stairs, Mr Martin realised he had forgotten to instruct the fellow to keep his mouth shut, but on reflection decided it would have been a waste of breath. He rather fancied the man would say nothing.

He found that Mrs Munch had kindled a fire in one of the small bedrooms at the top of the stairs and a sorely-tried Munch was toiling up and down the stairs with as much hot water as he could procure.

His lordship laid Mrs Bascombe on the bed, pulled back his coat to check his bandages were still in place, and decided there was nothing more to be done until the doctor should arrive. However long that would take.

Taking one look at the dim light that barely penetrated the small casement windows, Mr Martin disappeared in search of candles. Having delivered these, he found himself despatched to Westfield, in case Roberts had not yet found the doctor, and to bring back suitable assistance.

Mrs Munch was plying the bellows to get the flames going to her satisfaction. Heaving herself off her knees, she demanded of no one in particular to know what the world was coming to and began to tear a sheet into bandages. That done, she piled them ready on the bedstand and began to light the extra candles. Munch was despatched to heat yet more water.

Mrs Bascombe, looking very small and white on the faded bedcover, lay quietly, her eyes closed.

Apart from the crackling fire, the room was very quiet.

Roberts, it seemed, had found the doctor at home and to his lordship's relief, he appeared in the doorway some twenty minutes later. Lord Ryde described what had happened, indicated Mrs Bascombe upon the bed, informed the doctor he would be downstairs if required and withdrew to find the brandy.

Mr Martin, meanwhile, was on the road to Westfield. He found the place easily enough. The sight of a total stranger galloping up the avenue at such a speed was enough to bring Porlock to the door unsummoned. Long experience of Mrs Bascombe and her own individual style of riding had long since left him expecting the worst every time she left the house. When he learned, however, that she had been the victim of a shooting, he was very much shocked.

'I will summon Miss Fairburn,' he said, and having provided Mr Martin with very welcome refreshment, disappeared.

Mr Martin's experience of female companions was based on his Aunt Augusta's terrifying Miss Connor – part woman, part basilisk – and so his expectations of a female dragon were more than confounded when he found himself confronting a woman, very nearly his own height, with a creamy skin, dark hair, and bright eyes. She was simply dressed in a quiet fawn morning gown with a pink sprigged sash. Another woman would instantly have recognised her clothes as well-made, but home-made.

She listened quietly to his account of events, neither screaming nor fainting, although she caught her breath a little and her eyes widened. To his enormous relief, although undoubtedly alarmed, she showed no signs of hysteria or panic,

Thanking him somewhat disjointedly, she seemed to think for a moment and then, to his surprise, began to question him closely as to the domestic arrangements pertaining at Ryde House. That these did not meet her approval was immediately apparent.

A series of instructions were rattled off to Porlock, who immediately left the room.

'No, I'm sorry, ma'am,' protested Mr Martin, aghast at this departure from his lordship's instructions. 'There is no time. We must set off immediately.'

38

He paused to consider, briefly, that he and his lordship had travelled the length and breadth of Europe and beyond, with never so much as a servant between them for much of the time, although that was, admittedly, usually due to straightened circumstances, rather than by choice, but that was not the point.

Through the open door into the hall, he could see boxes, baskets, cases, and all sorts of female apparatus piling up. Truly, the amount of paraphernalia required by the average female taking to the road was astonishing. Mr Martin had no difficulty in imagining Lord Ryde, who had very little patience for this sort of thing, pitching the whole lot straight back out of the door. He regarded the growing heap with misgiving. When the heap was augmented by three additional females, each dressed in her outdoor clothes and showing every sign of being included in what was rapidly becoming an expedition, he threw convention to the winds and appealed to his fellow man.

Porlock, however, was unmoved by this piteous entreaty.

'It is Miss Fairburn's opinion,' he soothed, 'and mine as well, that the addition of herself and Mrs Bascombe to his lordship's bachelor establishment will place an intolerable strain on such domestic arrangements as are in place. And if, as you tell me, Mrs Bascombe is seriously injured and will require careful nursing then I think it fair to say that Mrs Munch – excellent woman though she is – will not prove equal to the task.'

Mr Martin, who had strong recollections of several meals over the last few days when Mrs Munch had not proved equal to the task, was very struck by this argument. He was a man who enjoyed his food. He suspected that Lord Ryde, notoriously indifferent to what was put in front of him anyway, was using each of the many discomforts of Ryde House as an excuse to leave as quickly as possible. Sometimes, Mr Martin thought, he seemed to look for reasons to hate his family home. And he was certainly never

one for cluttering up the place with a lot of females anyway
– at least not this sort of female, thought Mr Martin, eyeing
the more-than-respectable Margaret, just now tying her
bonnet strings. He became aware that everyone was
watching him expectantly.

Mr Martin, who had faced outlaws in the Pyrenees, street
gangs in Rome, and a Greek grandmother who was
mistakenly under the impression Lord Ryde had agreed to
marry her granddaughter, began to feel a little harassed.
With some idea of enlisting a kindred spirit, he looked
around for Miss Fairburn, who had disappeared. He was
punished for his inattention. While his back was turned, yet
another female had joined the group. And this one did look
like the dragon of his imaginings. They stared at each other.

'Er – good afternoon?' he hazarded.

Porlock sailed smoothly forwards.

'Allow me to introduce you, sir. This is Tiller, Mrs
Bascombe's maid. And this is Margaret, our head
housemaid; Eliza, our kitchen maid, and Janet from the
laundry. I trust you will find them all perfectly satisfactory,
sir.'

'No. Wait …' said Mr Martin, well aware of what his
lordship would say when he arrived at Ryde House towing
five females. And where the devil would he put them all
anyway? Mr Martin, as cool-headed under fire as anyone
could wish, now caught between five females on one hand
and Lord Ryde on the other, almost began to wish the bullet
had found him instead.

Hearing the sound of hooves and wheels outside, Porlock
flung open the doors to reveal two carriages. Immediately,
the baggage was dragged outside to be loaded. To Mr
Martin's eyes, it looked as if a small army was about to
invade. A not-inappropriate simile. However, he did
recognise one face. Roberts, seeing him at the top of the
steps, came forward and touched his hat.

'You found the doctor, then?' said Mr Martin, in relief.

Roberts nodded. 'Should be there by now, sir.'

'Good man.'

'Ah.'

They both stood together, possibly for mutual support, while a sea of women ebbed and flowed around them, with Porlock directing operations.

Miss Fairburn appeared, dressed for travel and added yet more boxes.

Mr Martin hailed her arrival with relief.

'Miss Fairburn, I really don't think …' he began.

She broke off from instructing Roberts to place Mrs Bascombe's dressing-case *inside* the coach and smiled, and Mr Martin, who had already had a trying afternoon and was, perhaps, a little more susceptible than he knew, blinked and then smiled back.

They stood like this for a while until the sudden absence of noise caused them to look around. All the baggage was loaded and all the females had climbed aboard. Roberts had mounted his horse and everyone was looking at them.

Mr Martin blushed deeply. 'May I assist you, ma'am?'

She gave him her hand and climbed into the first carriage. He slammed the door and turned to find himself face to face with Porlock, who, how that everything was safely in hand, allowed himself to show a little of the anxiety consuming him.

'Please take care of our Mrs Bascombe, sir,' he said, quietly.

'I will,' promised Mr Martin. He cast a glance behind him. 'I'll take care of all of them.'

A lesser man than Porlock might have had a twinkle in his eye. 'Good luck, sir.'

'Yes,' said Mr Martin, with feeling. 'Thank you.'

He mounted his horse and moved to the head of the column. Roberts took up position at the rear.

Porlock and an elderly woman, the housekeeper presumably, waved. The females all waved back. Goodbyes were shouted. Handkerchiefs fluttered.

They must be going all of four miles, reflected Mr Martin, who remembered crossing a flooded Rhine in a snowstorm with less fuss. And definitely with fewer women.

Back at Ryde House, Lord Ryde had barely settled himself in the library when Munch appeared to summon him back upstairs. Mrs Munch, it seemed, whilst perfectly happy to hold bowls and tear bandages, had found herself unable to take a more active part in the proceedings. Mrs Bascombe, feverish and restless, required gentle restraint.

The afternoon was drawing in and Mrs Munch had found it necessary to light even more candles. Mrs Bascombe lay, bathed in light, her wound exposed. The doctor, a short, dark, melancholy Welshman with his sleeves rolled up ready, directed his lordship to hold her still.

Lord Ryde, remembering he had at least been born a gentleman, averted his eyes and made a small gesture of protest, but Dr Jacobs, a grizzled veteran of several such accidents in this sporting neighbourhood shrugged and said there was no help for it.

'I cannot wait any longer, my lord, and Mrs Munch could probably not hold her in any case. If not you, then it must be Munch.'

His lordship gritted his teeth, but with every appearance of calm, seated himself on the other side of the bed and firmly grasped Mrs Bascombe's arms.

The doctor approached. 'Hold the light higher, Mrs Munch. That's it. Do you have water and towels ready? Then we shall begin.'

The next ten minutes were not pleasant. Mrs Bascombe opened her eyes to find Lord Ryde smiling encouragingly at her. By dint of keeping her eyes firmly on his and her teeth clenched, she bore it as best she could, until, at the very end, a particularly sharp spasm caused her to utter a cry of pain and twist in his lordship's grasp.

42

'I have it,' announced the doctor, dropping an object into Mrs Munch's bowl with a metallic clatter. 'All done, ma'am. I just need to dress the wound which looks perfectly clean to me and then we will leave you in peace. Thank you, my lord, that will do.'

He turned away, as he spoke.

Lord Ryde, gazing down upon Mrs Bascombe, white and exhausted, whispered, 'Good girl,' and let himself quietly out of the room.

He was descending the stairs in search of brandy – a great deal of brandy, actually – when he heard the clatter of hooves outside.

Munch, temporarily abandoning his water-carrying duties, trod less than majestically to the front door to admit Mr Martin and what seemed to an already-harassed Lord Ryde, an enormous number of women. Where the devil could they all have come from? His lordship tried to imagine Charles, the third son of a respectable clergyman in Gloucestershire, losing his head and driving madly around the countryside, scooping up every woman he could find.

Transfixed, he stood on the stairs and watched his friend – who would be accounting for this aberration very, very shortly – usher in a tall, dark lady, clad in a dove grey pelisse and bonnet with pink ribbons. Miss Fairburn, he assumed.

Miss Fairburn was followed by another tall woman, with a thin pointed face, dressed as a lady's maid – what was her name? Sir William had mentioned it – Tiller, that was it. Who was in turn followed by three – three, no less, count them – younger girls with the appearance of servants. While Miss Fairburn stripped off her gloves and looked around her, the most senior of the servants was directing the disposal of a number of cases, boxes, bags, and other impedimenta of unknown, but certainly sinister purpose.

Following all this, hat in hand, came Roberts, adrift in a sea of feminine bullying. Directed to carry a number of boxes to the kitchen regions, he disappeared with relief.

43

His lordship, wishing he could do the same, descended to the hall to defend his home.

'Ah, my lord,' said Mr Martin, himself appearing somewhat harassed. 'May I introduce Miss Laura Fairburn. Miss Fairburn, Lord Ryde.'

Miss Fairburn, far from uttering a shriek of maidenly terror at the sudden appearance of one whom she must have heard referred to in the same terms as the bogeyman, held out a hand and announced herself pleased to make his acquaintance.

'I must thank you, my lord. Mr Martin has been telling us that if not for your prompt action, Mrs Bascombe could – would – have died. We are all so grateful to you.'

Her voice was clear and calm and she appeared both competent and efficient. Here, obviously, was someone to whom he could relinquish the care of Mrs Bascombe with a clear conscience. However …

He regarded the trio of younger females and all the apparatus with misgivings. 'Who is "we all"?' he enquired.

Before she could reply, however, clanking keys announced the arrival of Mrs Munch. Even his lordship, no expert in Domestic Strife, could see that she was not happy. Fortunately for him, Miss Fairburn could take Domestic Strife in her stride.

'Mrs Munch, how do you do,' she said, moving past his lordship. 'I'm so sorry, this must have been a terrible upset for you. We are so grateful. Mr Porlock sends his compliments and has instructed us – most firmly – that we are not, under any circumstances, to make any extra work for you, and to that end, has despatched Margaret, our head housemaid, you know, to assist you with all the additional duties Mrs Bascombe's stay will entail. And here is Janet, our laundry maid and Eliza, the kitchen maid – all here to help you in every way. And Roberts is here too, to run errands and take messages should they be required. In fact,' she smiled warmly upon the speechless Mrs Munch, 'Mr

Porlock says you are to do nothing at all. You are to regard yourself as being at the very heart of the operation – the General, so to speak – not concerning yourself with the day-to-day tasks in any way, but sending out your instructions and taking command.'

His lordship wondered whether Porlock or Miss Fairburn herself was responsible for these astonishing instructions and then realised it was unimportant. He was not surprised to find Mrs Bascombe surrounded herself with other intelligent people.

Mrs Munch, on whom these words had worked like a charm, nodded in what she obviously imagined was a General-like fashion and led the way to the nether regions. The three maids obediently followed her, but not before Margaret and Miss Fairburn had exchanged a long, cool look. His lordship strongly suspected that Mrs Munch could order and direct and command as much as she pleased, but that control of the household now lay in the hands of the capable Margaret and the slightly frightening Miss Fairburn.

He turned to address Mr Martin and found his secretary staring at Miss Fairburn with an expression he had never seen before. His lordship sighed. Life had been so much simpler before Mrs Bascombe had contrived to get herself shot.

His hall was rapidly emptying. Luggage was being distributed and Mr Martin was escorting Miss Fairburn and Tiller upstairs. There being work to do, Munch had, as usual, vanished. Even as he looked, the last door closed and he was alone.

Gratefully, he made his way to the drawing room and poured out a brandy. Stretching himself comfortably in a battered leather armchair, he raised a glass to the portrait of his late father, the fourth Lord Ryde, hanging above the fireplace. He forgot now who the artist was, but it was counted to be one of his best works. His lordship could attest to that. So lifelike was his late lordship's familiar look of haughty contempt that one of Lord Ryde's first actions had been to have the picture moved from the library where he and Mr Martin often sat in the evenings, to the less-used drawing room. His lordship reflected that should he ever, for any reason, choose to make Ryde House his permanent home, the portrait's next resting place would be a distant attic.

He was just pouring himself another brandy when Munch ushered in the doctor. His lordship poured another glass which the doctor accepted with thanks. Waving him to a seat, Lord Ryde enquired after Mrs Bascombe.

'A clean wound, my lord. Mrs Bascombe has lost a great deal of blood, but I anticipate no permanent harm. She is strong and all should heal as it should.'

He peered at Lord Ryde from beneath heavy brows.

'I see your lordship has thought to bring over some of the Westfield people. An excellent notion, for I'll be bound it would be too much for your lordship's current – resources.'

Since he was reluctant to come straight out and ask when Mrs Bascombe would be able to travel and he could have his house back, Lord Ryde sought for a more acceptable form to this important question.

The doctor answered it before he could frame a suitable enquiry. 'The next few days might be tricky, but if there is no fever, she should be up and around in four or five days. She should be fit to return to Westfield in a se'ennight.'

His lordship rightly guessed that although there had been no choice in the matter, the removal of Mrs Bascombe to his bachelor establishment, even with the chaperonage of Miss Fairburn was causing the good doctor some concern. He said suddenly, 'Would it aid Mrs Bascombe's … recovery … if Mr Martin and I were to remove to – say, Rushford? Although I have to say, since I've come for the express purpose of looking into estate business, it would be devilish inconvenient.'

Dr Joseph frowned. 'Well, that was the other thing I

wanted to talk to you about, my lord. Mrs Bascombe's groom gave me the story of what happened and I don't scruple to say I'm shocked and appalled. If you choose to make up a story of careless poachers then that's your concern, sir, but I think we must, however unbelievable it may seem, put our minds towards considering the attack may have been deliberate. In other words, someone deliberately set out to do Mrs Bascombe harm. If that is indeed the case, my lord, I for one would feel a great deal easier in my mind knowing that you and Mr Martin are to continue here for the time being. Just in case, you understand.'

'You are presumably better acquainted with Mrs Bascombe than I, doctor. Just how likely is such an occurrence?'

'As I said, my lord, unbelievable. I do not consider the lady to have an enemy in the world. I do not know when I have been more shocked. However, I have given full instructions to Miss Fairburn, whom I believe more than equal to the task. You need not fear to find yourself surrounded by excitable females, my lord. In fact, I would not be surprised if they –' And there the doctor broke off, suddenly realising the discourtesy of criticising his lordship's apparently very casual living conditions and continued, 'I have given Mrs Bascombe something that will make her sleep for the rest of the day and probably most of the night. Fever and infection are the main dangers. If you have any concerns, send word and I'll come at once. I'll call tomorrow anyway. Afternoon probably, when the patient will almost certainly be awake. Good day to you, my lord.'

So saying, he drained his glass, bowed in a perfunctory manner and stumped away, leaving Lord Ryde to pour himself a second brandy and spend some time staring reflectively into the fire where he was found some time later by Mr Martin, who reported all the domestics were safely billeted, Miss Fairburn allocated a room adjacent to Mrs Bascombe's, ruffled feathers smoothed and peace (or inertia) had once more descended upon Ryde House.

'And I've sent a groom to Sir William Elliott, the local JP – you met him the other day – to apprise him of events here. He's away from home at the moment. I daresay we'll hear from him before too long, but I'll wager we hear from his wife first.'

Lord Ryde stared accusingly at his secretary. 'I wish you would consider my reputation before inviting every female in the neighbourhood to consider herself at home here.'

'I'll try to take more care in future,' apologised Mr Martin, meekly. Pouring himself a brandy, he sank into the chair lately vacated by the doctor and said, 'I've been thinking.'

'So have I,' admitted Lord Ryde. 'You go first, Charles.'

'Well, sir, I have to say, if I hadn't been there and seen it with my own eyes, I wouldn't have credited a word of it. It's incredible. A respectable woman shot and wounded practically on her own doorstep while going about her own business. Whatever next?'

His indignation caused Lord Ryde to smile.

Mr Martin continued. 'I mean, this is England. If we were back in the Pyrenees, or that place just outside Rome – do you remember? Or even that time in Prague – yes, I know we agreed never to mention it again – but sir, this is England. Rushfordshire. Nothing ever happens here.'

He fell silent, remembering that something had indeed happened here, in Rushford, in England on That Night, but his lordship, still staring into the fire, paid no heed.

'That's just it, Charles. Even setting aside the fact that there can hardly be anyone in the county at whom she has not aimed that horse at one time or another, who would want to shoot a respectable widow?'

Mr Martin started. 'Perhaps, my lord, that was the plan. To kill Mrs Bascombe and take possession of Westfield.'

'Westfield belongs to George Bascombe. Wherever he is. If he's still alive.'

'Maybe George Bascombe's dead and this is his heir trying to get rid of her.'

'I wish you would stop reading romantic novels,' complained his lordship. 'They really are affecting your ability to think properly. No wonder sensible mamas forbid them to their sensitive and impressionable daughters. If Bascombe's dead then his heir has only to drive up to the front door and present himself. Mrs Bascombe has no legal claim to Westfield whatsoever.'

Silence fell as both men stared into the fire. At length, Mr Martin stirred. 'In that case, my lord …'

'Yes?'

'No, it's ridiculous.'

'Well, say it anyway.'

'Well, I have to say, my lord. If not Mrs Bascombe, then the bullet must have been meant …'

'For me,' finished Lord Ryde.

'But that's …'

'That's what? Incredible? Impossible? Unbelievable? Haven't we just used all those words to describe the shooting of Mrs Bascombe? Is it more or less amazing that the target should have been me?'

'Frankly, sir, if we were still abroad, I might agree with you. Some of the scrapes you got us into – remember that Comtessa in Seville?'

'Vividly. I think we might add that to the list of things to forget as well, Charles, if you don't mind.'

'Of course, sir, but what I wanted to say was, why travel to England to put a bullet in you when it could have been done very much more easily and simply on the Continent? I know Boney's gone now, but it's still chaos over there.'

'I have enemies in England, too, you know,' said his lordship, indignantly.

'No doubt, sir,' replied Mr Martin soothingly. 'But can you think of any who would have been prepared to wait twenty years for your return? Even supposing they know of it. We told no one of your plans.'

His lordship paused and reviewed.

'Not really. Reeth, I suppose would be the main contender, but he died three, no, four years ago. There may be other husbands, of course, but devil take it, Charles, they'll be as old as I am, if not older. And don't start harping on about my creditors because it wouldn't suit them at all to see me dead.'

'Well, what about your heir, my lord?'

'Captain Francis Ryde is happily ensconced with his regiment abroad, a career soldier who prays daily for my continued well-being because he loathes this place nearly as much as I do.'

'Oh. That's disappointing.'

A brief flash of amusement crossed his lordship's harsh features.

'As you say, Charles, most disappointing. A murderous heir would have solved all our problems, I agree. Let's not despair, however. We may find, on closer investigation that Captain Ryde has recently become enamoured of a young lady and feels the acquisition of a gloomy old barrack of a house and any number of badly farmed acres are just what's needed for his beloved to look more favourably on his suit.'

Mr Martin grinned reluctantly. 'You may laugh, sir ...'

'I may. And I am. Laughing, that is. But that's only because I have the honour of knowing Captain Ryde and you, sadly, don't. And the clincher, Charles – he's a crack shot. At that range he could not have missed. No, I think we must return to considering Mrs Bascombe as the intended victim. Which makes me wonder – her homicidal riding habits aside – why would anyone want to kill Mrs Bascombe?'

Chapter Four

Being a bachelor establishment, neither gentlemen ever bothered to change for dinner and so they remained quietly in the library, whiling away the time by reading the newspapers sent up from London, speculating idly on the date of Mrs Bascombe's departure and in Lord Ryde's case, gloomily studying some sheets of figures his agent, Reynolds, had left for his perusal.

The library doors being both substantial and well made, they were unaware of even the smallest indication of the domestic upheaval occurring on the other side, and it was not until Munch, summoning them to his lordship's dismal dining room to partake of one of Mrs Munch's substantial but uninspired repasts, that the full horrors of a houseful of underemployed but determined females were brought home to his lordship.

Making his way across the hall towards the dining room, Lord Ryde halted abruptly on the threshold – so abruptly that Mr Martin all but walked into him. His lordship raised his quizzing glass and surveyed the appalling scene laid out before him.

'Good Lord,' said Mr Martin, softly.

His lordship had become accustomed, since his arrival at Ryde House, to two types of gloom. There was the sort of gloom that mercifully obscured all four corners of whichever room he happened to find himself in, and then there was the other type of gloom, signifying despair and dismay. Gazing now at his transformed dining room, his lordship could think of many words, but gloom was not any of them.

The chandelier had been unwrapped and lighted, throwing out a golden glow; the light reflected softly in the wooden panelling with which the room was generously provided. The old crimson and gold carpet had certainly been taken up and beaten. His lordship knew how it felt. The furniture gleamed and the whole room now smelled of beeswax and polish, rather than of dust and stale mouse droppings. The cloth was laid, the silver sparkled and light winked from the polished glasses. It was a sight to gladden any man's heart. His lordship's heart remained obstinately unglad.

'What the devil?' he exploded.

The retainer Munch, shuffling forwards, gave his employer to understand it was nothing to do with him.

'There were three of them,' he said, defensively. 'I told them straight – his lordship won't like it, I said. His lordship don't like to see things changed, he don't. I told 'em, his lordship'll have you gone in less time than the cat can lick her ear for your meddling, presumptuous ways and damn me if they don't just tie up their hair, push me – *me* – aside, and you never saw such a flurry of dusting and sweeping and I told them it would have to be done in time for his lordship's dinner and that Margaret sent me – *me* – for the stepladder – *me* – what's worked here all these years and worked my fingers to the bone, that's what I done, but no one took no notice and now see what's come of it.'

He paused in evident satisfaction and expectation that his employer would, with one powerful bound, rid the house of extraneous females, miraculously restore dust and grime, and the world would be as he had always known it.

'You have to admit, sir,' said Mr Martin, 'it does look – better.'

That it did indeed look better, his lordship would admit. That Munch's disapproval was rooted in the fear that after these damned – dashed – women had departed, he would be obliged to maintain these standards, his lordship had no doubt. He was half inclined to demand the presence of the three perpetrators and give them to understand their place in the scheme of things at Ryde House, and half inclined (out of sheer devilment) to let things go. Wholly aware that he was very hungry, he waved Munch aside and took his place at the head of the table. Mr Martin, slightly disappointed at this mild reaction, joined him.

However, by the end of the first course, which was removed with a baked ham and a game pie which both gentlemen devoured with relish, Lord Ryde had mellowed to the extent of being prepared to allow the miscreants to remain under his roof a while longer. With the guarantee that no further outrages would occur.

An enquiry as to Miss Fairburn's dining arrangements brought the information that the lady had enjoyed a tray in Mrs Bascombe's room. Mrs Bascombe herself was still asleep and therefore could not, theoretically, be held responsible for the assault on his lordship's dining room.

'My compliments to Miss Fairburn. Please inform her we would be delighted if she would join us for tea.'

A weakened Munch reeled before this fresh horror.

'Your lordship wants a … tea-tray?'

'Yes, immediately, please. Miss Fairburn will not want to leave Mrs Bascombe for too long.'

Muttering darkly, Munch disappeared, to re-appear, eventually and simultaneously with the despised object and Miss Fairburn herself.

His lordship, beyond rising and bowing, left Mr Martin to seat his guest and pour the tea.

Mrs Bascombe, she reported, was still sleeping quietly. Yes, she, Miss Fairburn, had eaten, thank you, as had Tiller. They were preparing to divide the night between them.

Lord Ryde spoke for the first time.

'The doctor did not anticipate that Mrs Bascombe would pass anything other than a peaceful night, Miss Fairburn. However, should anything occur to cause you alarm, you may rouse either myself or Mr Martin. We will leave lamps outside our doors. Pray do not bother ringing for Munch. Mr Martin's opinion is that he falls into a coma at midnight from which nothing short of a naval salute will rouse him.'

She smiled.

'Thank you, my lord. And on behalf of Mrs Bascombe as well, thank you.'

His lordship waved this aside.

She hesitated, staring down into her teacup. 'I wonder, my lord, have you formed any theories – do you have any idea – how this could possibly have happened?'

'As a stranger to the district, Miss Fairburn, I am at a loss. If any of your neighbours harbour murderous intentions, surely you would know that better than I.'

Miss Fairburn, suspecting his lordship of sarcasm, took him at his word.

'Well, let me see. There are the Misses Crosby at Crosby Lodge. Sixty-seven and sixty-nine years old, respectively, but I have sometime suspected ... Miss Amelia, you know, sometimes has a very strange look about her, and her way of gliding through the rose gardens, silver scissors raised, has more than once caused comment. And then there's Sir Timothy Relton. Who knows to what lengths he might be driven when his gout is troubling him. And Mr and Mrs Brookes, out at Fern Park – she is a great deal taken up with their numerous offspring and it's well known that Mr Brookes rarely ventures out of his library, but their eldest child – a delightful cherub of around nine, is, I believe, something of a handful and I, for one, have always maintained that these angel-faced children can often conceal a sinister ...'

'Yes, ma'am,' interrupted Lord Ryde, with an answering gleam in his eye. 'I believe you have made your point. This is a neighbourhood of unimpeachable respectability.'

'Well, it is,' replied Miss Fairburn, somewhat wistfully, Mr Martin thought.

'Do you have any theories yourself, Miss Fairburn?' he asked her, curiously.

'Well, if not a poacher, as I believe has been suggested, then I would say perhaps young boys, out with their father's gun. Taken without his permission, of course, and now they would be too ashamed and frightened to own up.'

'Why, ma'am, I believe that may be it.'

She sighed. 'Alas, sir, the only possible culprits could be the Jamieson boys and they not only live out near Whittington, but are, I believe, at school.'

'Even so,' said Mr Martin, eagerly, 'it could have been a farmer's son, or any of the tradesmen's boys.'

'Let us hope that that is the case,' said his lordship, gravely.

She watched his face carefully. 'You don't agree, my lord?'

'I have no more information than anyone else. Now, do you have everything you need for the night?'

'Yes, indeed, my lord. We are very comfortably housed.'

His lordship doubted this.

'Remember, if you need anything in the night, you have only to knock on our doors.'

She set down her cup and rose. 'Thank you, my lord. I wish you goodnight.'

'I'll see you to your room,' said Mr Martin, holding the door for her.

On entering Mrs Bascombe's room, Miss Fairburn was relieved to find her patient still sound asleep. Releasing Tiller to catch a few hours' sleep, she settled herself in an uncomfortable armchair by the fire and prepared herself for a long night.

She heard the gentlemen come to bed, talking quietly as they mounted the stairs. She heard their doors close and felt silence envelop the old house. For an hour or so, all was still. She leaned her head back against the chair and closed her eyes.

55

She was awakened from a light doze by a faint sound from the bed. And then another. Mrs Bascombe was awake. Miss Fairburn picked up the candle and stole quietly to the bed. She was alarmed to see her friend, flushed and tousled in the faint light, plucking at her bandages. She managed to pull her hand away and at her command, Mrs Bascombe closed her eyes.

Minutes later, she was awake again, tossing on her pillows and murmuring incomprehensibly. Responding again to her friend's voice, she subsided back into an uneasy slumber.

This did not last long, however, and she awoke some thirty minutes later with a feverish torrent of words. Miss Fairburn applied cold cloths to her forehead and endeavoured to bring her to her senses, but to no avail. Miss Fairburn had no hesitation in calling for Tiller who tersely recommended the doctor be sent for.

Miss Fairburn could not but agree. Reluctantly picking up a candle, she tip-toed along the darkened corridor. It seemed logical to assume that the big double doors at the end gave into his lordship's room and Miss Fairburn, despite his assurances to the contrary, was reluctant to wake him. Mr Charles Martin seemed a much friendlier option.

Tapping gently on the nearest door, she was reassured to hear the sound of curtain rings as the bed curtains were pulled back, but seconds later, the door opened and she was disconcerted to find herself face to face with a magnificently dressing-gowned Lord Ryde.

Whilst a corner of her mind registered surprise that he did not, if fact, appear to occupy his father's room, she lost no time in telling him of her anxieties and requesting in a low voice, that the doctor be sent for.

'I have some experience of this sort of fever,' he said quietly. 'Before we trouble the doctor, will you permit me to see her?'

Comforting herself with the thought that no one would

ever know, and rather glad to devolve responsibility, even if only for a moment, Miss Fairburn gladly assented.

Mrs Bascombe's condition had worsened during this brief absence and even Tiller made no demur at his lordship's entrance.

Lord Ryde regarded Mrs Bascombe for a moment, before enquiring if the doctor had left anything against this eventuality.

'He did, my lord,' said Miss Fairburn, indicating a small bottle, resting on the bedstand, 'but neither of us can hold her still enough to drink it.'

'I think we can remedy that. Pour out the draught, Tiller. Miss Fairburn, if I hold her still – can you be ready?'

Accepting the glass from Tiller, Miss Fairburn stood ready.

'You will need to be quick,' he warned. 'She will not take it willingly.'

'I am ready, sir.'

Lord Ryde lifted Mrs Bascombe from the bed and gently but firmly held her against his shoulder.

Miss Fairburn advanced

'Mrs Bascombe,' said his lordship commandingly. 'Elinor. Look at me.'

Mrs Bascombe ceased to struggle, looked up, and opened her mouth to speak. Quick as a flash, Miss Fairburn tipped the liquid down her throat. Mrs Bascombe uttered a squawk of outrage and struggled again. His lordship held her firmly until slowly, her struggles subsided and she grew heavy in his arms. Slowly, her eyelids drooped and she fell asleep again.

'I will wait a few minutes. Is there another dose, just in case?'

'I am afraid not, sir. The doctor would only leave enough for one. It is very strong, apparently.'

And indeed, Mrs Bascombe was lying on her bed like one poleaxed. A slight snore could be heard.

His lordship's lip twitched.

'I will leave you now, ladies. I don't think Mrs Bascombe will stir again tonight. Miss Fairburn, I hope you will join us at breakfast tomorrow to apprise me of Mrs Bascombe's condition.'

He bowed in the general direction of both ladies and quitted the rom.

Tiller announced she would remain for the rest of the night, and Miss Fairburn, more tired than she would admit, went thankfully to her bed.

She had intended to mull over the events of this strange day, and to speculate about Mr Charles Martin and a Lord Ryde who apparently disliked his father so much that he would not even sleep in his bedroom, but fell asleep as soon as her head touched the lumpy pillow.

She woke the next morning with a stiff neck and back and a longing for the comfort of Westfield. She supposed his lordship to be blind to these discomforts – any gentleman who had racketed around the globe for the last twenty years was not going to be greatly disturbed by a lumpy bed and musty bed sheets. There was no escaping the fact, however, that Ryde House was a dreary place and the sooner Mrs Bascombe was restored to the warmth and comfort of Westfield, the better it would be for all concerned.

And as for permitting Lord Ryde to enter her bedchamber during the night, to manhandle an unconscious (or as good as) Mrs Bascombe whilst in a state of undress himself – Miss Fairburn blushed hotly and prayed her part in the events of last night would never become known.

Entering the dining room half an hour later, she was able to report that Mrs Bascombe had spent a peaceful night. From the remarks made by Mr Martin, she was reassured to find his lordship did not appear to have mentioned his nocturnal visit and found herself warming towards him. It might be a mistake, she told herself, to accept his lordship at other people's valuation.

Both gentlemen were regarding their breakfast board with astonishment and in Mr Martin's case, with reverence. Miss Fairburn, perfectly accustomed to a choice of tea or coffee, fresh warm rolls and several varieties of fruit preserve, bit back a smile. This pedestrian fare was further augmented by slices of ham, beef, and the remains of last night's game pie. Munch, observing Margaret moving smartly between table and board to supply the gentlemen's needs, oozed disapproval to which no one paid the slightest attention. Outside, the sun shone, birds sang, and inside, Lord Ryde enjoyed yet another cup of coffee from an apparently inexhaustible pot.

Embracing the part of disinterested friend with enthusiasm, he advised Miss Fairburn to take some exercise, saying that she would not be serving her friend by exhausting herself and recommending Mr Martin to show her the walk around the lake. A little overgrown in places, no doubt, but perfectly passable and a favourite walk of his mother's. A remark which surprised him as much as Mr Martin who had never before heard him refer to his mother. He would, however, come to regret this disinterested kindness.

To begin with, on exiting the dining room, he encountered a pair of female rumps and was so much astonished by this unexpected sight as to utter an astonished cry, at which one of the rumps giggled.

'What the dev – the deuce?' demanded his lordship, recovering the power of speech.

'I believe,' said Miss Fairburn, appearing in her bonnet and pulling on her gloves, 'that they are scrubbing the tiles, my lord.'

'I swear, Charles,' said his lordship in an undertone, 'if instead of bothering with an army, Bonaparte had just picked up half a dozen females instead, we would all be speaking French by now.'

'And they would have cleaned as they went along and we would dine on game pie every night,' grinned Mr Martin.

His lordship turned a cold eye upon him.

'You must not let me detain you, Charles.'

Mr Martin and Miss Fairburn made their escape into the fine morning sunshine.

Lord Ryde was again to regret his kindness. Unable to access the stairs for female obstruction, he withdrew to the library with instructions he was not to be disturbed, an instruction Munch claimed not to have heard as he ushered Lady Elliott into the room some twenty minutes later.

His lordship, sprawled coatless in front of the fire as was his wont, was caught unawares. Throwing his retainer a Look, he shrugged himself into his coat, once again thanking his lucky stars he was not some Bond Street beau, unable to don his own coat without the assistance of two strong men. Lady Elliot, who had debated long and hard with herself over the propriety of visiting a bachelor establishment without the support of her husband, watched all this with relieved amusement.

A parade of good manners and social address would have concerned her greatly. A tired-looking man shrugging himself into his shabby coat was not at all her idea of the dangerous and disreputable rake of whom she had heard so much. It was only as he walked towards her that she became aware that charm does not always present a glittering exterior.

'Good morning, ma'am. I believe I had the honour of meeting your husband the other day. I collect you have called to enquire after Mrs Bascombe.'

She pulled off her gloves and shook his hand with more cordiality than she had expected to feel. Gratitude there must be, of course – this man had saved her beloved Elinor. Liking, she had not expected to experience and was disconcerted.

His lordship, far more accustomed to the processes of the

female mind than he would admit, saw more than Lady Elliott ever dreamed. Biting back a smile, he informed her Miss Fairburn had taken advantage of Mrs Bascombe's still being asleep to take a little fresh air.

'For it would not do, ma'am, to have two invalids upon our hands,' he finished, straight-faced.

Lady Elliott, however, was no fool.

'It would certainly not do for you, my lord,' she said, tartly. 'I understand that these days, Ryde House positively bulges with females.'

'It is true, ma'am, that we no longer reap the benefits of a bachelor establishment.'

'One day, you must enumerate these benefits.'

'If you will be seated, ma'am, I will begin.'

'I find it difficult to believe it would take so long.'

He smiled, reluctantly. 'Can I ask Mrs Munch to conduct you to Mrs Bascombe's chamber?'

'That might be wise, my lord.'

Mrs Bascombe was still asleep, however, and after exchanging a few words with Tiller, Lady Elliott sat quietly to await the doctor, passing the time in silent criticism of Mrs Munch's standards of housekeeping and mentally refurbishing the shabby chamber in which she found herself.

Dr Joseph professed himself unconcerned by Mrs Bascombe's feverish night and had no hesitation in vetoing Lady Elliott's proposal to remove her at once, either to Westfield or to Greystones, her own establishment.

'I would not care to take the risk,' he advised, bluntly. 'I can guess your ladyship's concerns – the situation is far from ideal, but provided we can prevent any relapse, which we can by keeping the patient quiet and still for three or four days, with luck Mrs Bascombe could be home within a week. His lordship has volunteered to remove himself and Mr Martin to Rushford, but do you not feel, my lady, that the presence of Miss Fairburn and Miss Tiller, together with her three maids and her groom is enough to protect Mrs

Bascombe reputation from any untoward gossip that may occur? I for one, would feel much happier to have two gentlemen on the premises.'

Lady Elliott was by no means immune to that brief flash of elusive Ryde charm – so fleeting and so beguiling. What its effect might be on her wholly inexperienced friend was not a subject on which she wished to dwell. Lady Elliott was far from fearing Lord Ryde's impulses might get the better of him, but the sort of women he consorted with would all be familiar with the rules of the game. She felt it was very probable that even Ryde himself would be wholly unaware of his possible effect on Elinor's fragile, brittle heart.

She was a sensible woman, however, and what must be, must be. She followed the doctor downstairs to find Lord Ryde, far from scheming to lure Elinor into his nets of seduction, was dressed for riding and plainly only awaiting her departure before disappearing off on his own business.

His slightly bored enquiries were such as to convince Lady Elliott that he too was awaiting Mrs Bascombe's removal with barely controlled impatience. Perversely, she was conscious of a feeling of annoyance. She would have liked to discuss the circumstances of the shooting and followed his lordship down the steps to her carriage, resolving to instruct her husband to call at Ryde House immediately on his return from Rushford, wither he had repaired two days previously, on business.

Inwardly laughing, his lordship bade a punctilious farewell to a ruffled Lady Elliott and made haste across country to the scene of the previous day's incident.

Dismounting, he found Mr Martin already present, on his hands and knees, subjecting portions of the hedgerow to minute scrutiny.

'Anything, Charles?' he enquired.

Mr Martin rose to his feet and dusted himself down.

'Nothing that I can see, sir. There is evidence that someone stood just here for some considerable time, judging by the imprints in the soft ground. And here are one or two broken twigs that look quite fresh – but who stood here, and exactly when, and whether it was anything to do with Mrs Bascombe's shooting, I'm afraid I cannot say.'

'How the deuce did the fellow get away, then? There are no footprints anywhere that I can see.'

'Well, sir, if it was me, I would have made my way down the hedge, rather than across the field. There must be any number of small hiding places therein. So long as he kept his nerve and stayed quiet … and we, of course, were far too busy tending to Mrs Bascombe and fetching help.'

'Very neat,' agreed his lordship. 'Not the actions of a guilty poacher or frightened boys.'

'I fear not, my lord.'

'Well, well. A mystery. And probably, we shall never know.'

'You do not mean to prolong your stay at Ryde house, my lord?'

'To what purpose?'

'Well, aren't you the tiniest bit curious, sir? That such a thing could happen – here, of all places?'

'Charles, tell me seriously, do you mean to spend more days here than you have to, eating bad food, drinking indifferent wine and sleeping in devilishly draughty discomfort?'

'We've had worse, sir.'

'Yes, but we didn't have to call it home.'

'Even so, sir, we always planned to stay at least for a fortnight. It surely couldn't hurt to extend a few days?'

His lordship belatedly remembered Mr Martin's face as he beheld Miss Fairburn. He and Charles had been roaming erratically for as long he could remember. The length of their stays had ranged from nearly a year in Rome, to just under ten minutes in a sinister hostelry near Athens which had been presided over by a particularly villainous-looking proprietor, who had cast covetous eyes on their horses and a nastily calculating glance on their owners. He remembered they had left with all speed and spent that night wrapped in their cloaks under a rocky overhang some five miles up the road. And still been more comfortable than any time in his own ancestral pile, he reminded himself.

He shifted his weight and stared around. High, overgrown hedges surrounded rank pasture. The ground was still soft from the recent rain. Choked ditches meant bad drainage. And not just in this field. He had acres and acres of equally disheartened land. Tumbledown agricultural buildings, poor stock, outmoded farming methods. The world had moved on and left Ryde House behind. If it had been in his lordship's power, he would have razed it all to the ground years ago.

Chapter Five

Both gentlemen rode home lost in their own individual thoughts.

Those of Mr Martin were easy to divine. Those of Lord Ryde, less so. He had not missed that note of reluctance in Mr Martin's voice when he spoke of resuming their travels, although travels seemed too dignified a word for the erratic wanderings of the last twenty years or so.

Suppose Charles did refuse to accompany him when he departed Ryde House. As he could perfectly well do. Secretary he might call himself, but his position was far closer and more complex than that. They had met at university. Charles was several years his junior, the third son of an impecunious rector already financially exhausted through educating his two elder sons and providing dowries for his daughters. Opposites attract and an unlikely friendship developed after Mr Martin's timely intervention when a young Jack Ryde had once again bitten off more than he could chew in a narrow alleyway at the back of an establishment famed for the plucking of inexperienced young undergraduates.

Both young gentlemen had given excellent accounts of themselves and an enduring friendship had been born. Mr Martin was naturally Jack Ryde's choice as second on the occasion of that infamous meeting with Sir Matthew Reeth. It was his timely actions that had subsequently saved his friend's life. Exiled abroad by his father, Mr Ryde had no hesitation extending an invitation to an equally unhesitating Mr Martin. Mr Martin's father, seeing his third son provided for, raised no objections at all. Mr Ryde chose to dignify the position with the title 'secretary' and thus make his friend a small remuneration – some part of which he guessed, made its way back to the rectory in Gloucestershire.

The arrangement had worked very well and the two now not so young men had been drifting erratically around the continent, finding adventure, fortune, and disaster in equal measure, avoiding the various armies of the period and thoroughly enjoying their wildly fluctuating circumstances.

It now occurred to Lord Ryde, quite suddenly, that when he did finally shake off the dust with which Ryde House was so plentifully provided, that Mr Martin might not wish to accompany him. It was not his first attraction, of course, there had been that very pretty girl in Brussels; his lordship suspected though, that this might be his last. He had no doubt that should he specifically request him to do so, Mr Martin would follow him, but would he make that request? Should he? For the first time, he had to consider a future without his best friend. It would be cruel to drag Charles away from England if his heart was plainly elsewhere. He had a sudden, unwelcome vision of two ageing, homeless, rootless men, drifting aimlessly until accident or poor health caught up with them as it surely would do one day, unable to support themselves, eking out a pathetic existence in some shabby room somewhere until one died, leaving the other desolate and alone.

Perhaps Charles was right to think about settling down, and if that was truly what he wanted, Lord Ryde would do everything in his power to help him achieve his wish.

And what of himself? Would he continue his travels alone? The prospect held no appeal. He had a suspicion that what were enjoyable adventures when shared with a good friend would be in no way as enjoyable without him, but was the alternative any better? To settle at Ryde House with its cold, dark memories? To hear the name of Bascombe every day? To preside over decay and ruin?

Whatever decision he made would be irrevocable. If he

stripped the estate and set off again there would be no returning. Why would he ever want to? This was no happy home of his childhood. This was a constant reminder of his father's dislike. His disappointment in his only child. His preference for Georgie Bascombe. Who had murdered the father and impoverished the son.

And if he did return to his wanderings – with or without Charles. Where would he go? Where had they not yet been? What sights had they not yet viewed?

He roused himself from his reverie with some relief, to find himself approaching his own front door.

Mrs Bascombe woke not very long after Lady Elliott had departed, dragging herself free from the clinging tendrils of black memories. For a fleeting moment, she had imagined herself back in ... Fear, for so long her only friend, had returned to haunt her dreams. She lay very quietly and pieced together as much as she could remember of the previous day's happenings.

She found herself in an uncomfortable bed in a strange room. The pillows appeared to be made of bricks and the linen smelled musty. Correctly concluding she was not yet back at Westfield, her eyes wandered vaguely until she saw something she could recognise and said weakly, 'Tilly?'

Her maid, who had been awkwardly sweeping the hearth came swiftly to her side, crying, 'Oh, my dear. My dear Miss Elinor, you're awake at last.'

'I am indeed,' agreed Mrs Bascombe. 'And very thirsty. May I have some water, please?'

'Better than that,' said Tiller. 'Eliza has made lemonade.'

'Eliza? Our Eliza? Am I at Westfield, then? I don't understand?'

'Now, Miss Elinor, don't you fret yourself. You're at Ryde House, if you remember. We're all here to look after you. Miss Fairburn is here. She's out taking the air at present. And Margaret's here. Eliza and Janet too. Never you mind about anything, my dear. Now, let me help you sit up.'

Mrs Bascombe lay back on her lumpy pillows and took stock of her surroundings. Cheerless it might have been, but some efforts had been made to render the room more habitable.

The curtains were looped back from the windows and one casement had been forced open to let in a little air. A small fire burned cheerfully in the hearth. The battered and mismatched furniture consisted of a bed, minus its hangings, two chairs placed either side of the fireplace, a small table at the side of the bed, and a chest of drawers pushed against a wall.

In the centre of the room, however, stood a number of boxes. Mrs Bascombe, sipping her lemonade, watched as her maid unpacked the items she had hastily thrown together on Miss Fairburn's instructions. Mrs Bascombe took a small comfort from this familiar routine and Tiller could conceal her overwhelming joy and relief in bustling activity.

The dreadful old pillows were replaced with Mrs Bascombe's own, lace-edged and soft. The sheets could wait, but the faded quilt was removed, folded carefully, and stored away. Mrs Bascombe's own very pretty cream and blue quilt was gently spread across the bed instead. Her brushes and mirrors were placed on the chest of drawers and her dressing gown hung carefully beside the bed.

Miss Tiller itched to change Mrs Bascombe's current nightshirt – one of his lordship's, and very kindly meant, no doubt, but most inappropriate. And large. Very, very large. Even with the sleeves rolled back, they hung over Mrs Bascombe's small hands.

At the very bottom of the last box lay some half a dozen lavender bags, made by Miss Elinor herself. She tucked one inside the pillows, two into the drawers and hung the rest around the room. A familiar and reassuring smell permeated the room.

Mrs Bascombe, sipping her lemonade, watched all this

with a twinkle in her eye and requested the whereabouts of Lord Ryde. Miss Tiller thankfully professed herself unable to say and was at that moment undone by the sound of horses' hooves under her window and his lordship shouting for Owen, his groom.

Mrs Bascombe handed back her glass and requested a word with his lordship at his earliest convenience.

'Now that, Mrs Bascombe, if you don't mind me saying so, is just what you ought not to be doing. I'm not saying his lordship's behaviour hasn't been everything it should, because it has, and no one will deny he had no choice but to bring you here, and he done his duty like a Christian, but to be encouraging him to come to your room and you still in your bed is not what I hold with, and you shouldn't neither.'

Mrs Bascombe let her run down and then quietly repeated her request. Recognising the tone, Tiller withdrew, muttering, to pass on the message.

Some twenty minutes later, his lordship was received by Mrs Bascombe, still in her bed, admittedly, but modestly swathed in a pretty paisley shawl and with her hair dressed in a simple knot. Mrs Bascombe had complied with the shawl and the hair, but, as usual, drawn the line a wearing a cap. Admitting his lordship to Mrs Bascombe's room, Tiller withdrew to the window seat and picked up her whitework in such a way as to convey the impression it could easily be discarded, should she feel the necessity to leap to her mistress's defence.

A chair had been placed at a prim distance from the bed, and with one wary eye on the Gorgon in the window seat, his lordship seated himself and enquired of Mrs Bascombe how she did.

'Very well, thank you.'

Silence.

'Did you summon me for a reason?'

'Oh, dear. Did I seem to summon you? That was not my intention.'

His lordship, carefully not glancing at Tiller in any way, admitted to a poor choice of words.

Mrs Bascombe, too, could conciliate. 'Selfishly, sir, I have dragged you from your business to give myself the pleasure of expressing my gratitude. I have no need to ask what happened – I remember all of it,' she continued, without any particular emphasis. 'And so, Lord Ryde, not to keep you any longer, please allow me to say thank you.'

'You are entirely welcome, ma'am.'

Silence.

Experiencing again the curiosity that had so frequently led to periods of excitement and activity in his and Mr Martin's lives, his lordship ventured to enquire if she had any ideas about the identity of her attacker.

'None,' she said, frankly. 'Absolutely none. It must surely have been an accident and the perpetrator too afraid to come forward.'

Again, his lordship's mind went back to that moment – the bird, erupting from the hedgerow – the shrill cry of alarm – Rufus leaping sideways, to bring Mrs Bascombe between himself and the hedge … Inwardly, he shrugged. It was a poacher. It had to be. How could it be anything other? And frankly, did he care? A few days and she would be gone. And all the rest of that Monstrous Regiment with her. And in another week, so would he. With or without Charles, he would be gone. He could hire another secretary.

But not another friend, whispered a treacherous voice from somewhere deep inside.

'What is it?'

He refocused to find Mrs Bascombe staring at him in consternation.

'I'm sorry, what did you say?'

'Is something wrong, my lord? For a moment, you looked …'

'No,' he said, with something of an effort. Of course nothing is wrong. I believe we were discussing your

70

assailant.'

Mrs Bascombe regarded him carefully for a moment and then said, casually, 'Well, whoever it was, and for whatever reason it happened, it's finished now. And even if it's not, even if some blood-crazed lunatic does stalk the neighbourhood only awaiting another opportunity to murder me where I stand, when I return to Westfield, he will undoubtedly follow me there and you'll be safe, my lord. So there is no reason to feel any alarm. If you like, I can leave some of my people here, if it will make you and Mr Martin feel more secure.'

Lord Ryde was temporarily lost for words.

Mrs Bascombe smiled encouragingly. 'Fear not, my lord. We won't let anyone hurt you.'

Lord Ryde recovered the power of speech.

'Allow me to inform you, madam, that I accepted your thanks under false pretences. You owe your life solely to the efforts of Mr Martin, your groom, and a passing farmer. Left to myself, I would have stepped over you and ridden home with all speed.'

'That's the spirit,' she said approvingly. 'How much more agreeable it is to abuse a poor, sick widow than give way to the blue devils.'

'I can assure you, madam, that had I the slightest inkling of the identity of the man who shot you, I would be shaking him warmly by the hand.'

'As opposed to shaking me warmly by the throat, I suppose,'

'Shooting is too good for you, Mrs Bascombe. Should I ever experience the entirely understandable urge to murder you myself, believe me, ma'am, your ending will be both painful and slow.'

She shifted uncomfortably in her bed.

'Well, you have made a good start with the painful part.'

'I'm sorry,' he said quickly. 'We put you here because this room was nearest. I'm sure we could – probably – find

71

you somewhere more comfortable.'

'No, no. I should not have said that. I am so sorry. Whatever my stupid tongue says, I know I owe you my life and if I seemed ungrateful or ungracious, I am truly sorry for that, as well. To have me here must be enormously inconvenient and you have not uttered one word of complaint.'

His lordship, who had actually uttered a great many words of complaint, could not help smiling.

'There,' she said in small triumph. 'Much better.'

'Mrs Bascombe, you are the most manipulative, infuriating ...' he paused, searching for words.

'My lord,' she said softly, 'I would so much rather see you infuriated than sad.'

At this moment, however, benevolent Providence decreed Margaret's arrival with a tea tray. His lordship would have made good his escape, but found himself pressed into service, moving tables and passing the invalid her tea.

Elinor, still thirsty, needed no urging to drink her tea, although, with a twinkle in her eye, she declined the proffered plate of macaroons.

'You should eat,' said Lord Ryde, disposing of his tea and macaroons by simply putting them on the floor. 'Shall I have some broth sent up?'

'Thank you, but I'm more thirsty than hungry at the moment.'

'Would you like another cup?'

'Not just at the moment, thank you.'

'Well, I shall take my leave, then. I'm happy to see you sitting up and taking notice, Mrs Bascombe. Joking aside – both Charles and I wish you a speedy recovery.'

'Joking aside, my lord, thank you for my life. There – such a dramatic phrase, but, I suspect, perfectly true.'

She shivered.

'Do you fear to return to Westfield, ma'am? Do you have relations to whom I can apply for aid?'

'My family is so far away as to be useless, and in any event would not respond if I asked, which I won't do. So, I'm afraid, no. My friends are all here in this neighbourhood. I shall do very well, I assure you.'

'There must be someone.'

She hesitated, and then said with a certain deliberation, 'My nearest male relative, my lord, is George Bascombe. If you can find him.'

'I'm afraid if ever I do find him, Mrs Bascombe, I shall do everything within my power to bring him to justice.'

'Nothing is proved,' she said swiftly.

'Nothing needs to be. The facts speak for themselves,' he retorted, angrily.

'There must be some other explanation. A man – a boy, rather, because that's what he was – does not save a life one moment, only to take another, different life an hour or so later. It's nonsense. You must see that.'

Lord Ryde took Mrs Bascombe's cup and refilled it.

'Please drink this. I have upset you and such was not my intention.'

'She took the cup.

'I am not upset, sir. I have had many years to come to terms with this – but remember, I knew Georgie and you did not. There must be some other factor; something about which we know nothing. There has to be.'

The facts are simple, ma'am. After you were – after he was driven from Westfield, he sought refuge here, at Ryde House. I don't say he meant to do it, but the temptation was obviously too much for him. He was penniless, homeless – he had nothing. Later that night, my father was discovered, unconscious on the floor of the library. The safe door stood ajar. The safe was empty of anything valuable and George Bascombe was gone. No one has seen or heard from him since. The events of that night caused my father to have a stroke from which he never recovered and two weeks later, he died.

'I never liked him, ma'am, nor he me, but even so –' He broke off. 'I'm sorry, I didn't mean to distress you. Whether Bascombe's actions brought about the stroke, no one will ever know. Possibly, he suffered the stroke whilst Bascombe was actually present and he merely took advantage of my father's weakness to help himself from the safe and make good his escape. Whichever it was, he left an old man lying helpless on the floor and stole nearly everything he possessed. My father didn't believe in banks. He kept his possessions close so there was plenty to take away; my mother's jewels, including the family diamonds – hideous but valuable – cash boxes, the lot. My father could not have made it any easier for him. Including the jewels, he must have got away with the best part of £50,000.'

Mrs Bascombe gaped. In the window seat, Tiller had long ceased even to pretend to sew.

'It's one of the reasons you are housed in such discomfort today, ma'am. Blame George Bascombe. Oh, I've played my part, I know. For years, I've done nothing but take as much as I could get. That's why I'm here now – to strip the last flesh from the carcase, get out and never come back. So you need not fear I shall be polluting the district with my presence, ma'am. Once I have what I want, I shall never return.'

The silence in the room reverberated like a bell. Mrs Bascombe lay back, very pale indeed.

'Dear me,' said his lordship lightly. 'Did I just say all that? How very unfortunate. I make you my apologies, ma'am. Your very obedient servant.'

He swept from the room and finding himself disinclined for company, ran down the backstairs and out to the stables.

These were located at the rear of the main building, entered through an archway and formed round three sides of a square. Two of the sides had long ago been abandoned and locked up, but on the third side, doors stood open and showed signs of life. Lord Ryde, who remembered still the

74

days when, as a child, he had perched upon the mounting block and watched the noisy bustle around him, found himself experiencing a small pang to which he found no difficulty in ascribing to the wretched Mrs Bascombe. Pulling up short in the archway, he surveyed, as if for the first time, the weeds growing up through the cobbles, the peeling paint, the missing tiles, and the general air of dilapidation. Ryde House itself invoked no such feelings of regret, but here in this stableyard, many years ago, he had been happy.

The memories were fleeting and painful. He shook his head as Roberts took a step towards him, saying uncertainly, 'My lord?' turned on his heel and without any clear idea of what he was doing, walked somewhat blindly around to the front of the house. There he stood for a long time, his back to the building, surveying the abandoned gardens and overgrown lawns.

After a while, he turned to look at the house itself. Mr Martin, passing through the hall, caught sight of him through one of the widows, paused, and then moved on. Returning back the same way, half an hour later, he was surprised to see his lordship still standing on the weedy gravel, hands thrust deep into his breeches pockets – just standing.

Mr Martin watched thoughtfully for a while and upon his lordship turning to face towards the house, caught a glimpse of his face, and wished he hadn't. Ringing for Munch, he got Margaret instead, instructed her to warn everyone to stay out of sight for an hour or so and to take the brandy into the library. Being advised that the library was in a state of some upheaval, he amended that to the drawing room and warned her for God's sake to keep the library doors closed.

Margaret nodded, curtseyed, and silently withdrew.

Returning inside some time later, Lord Ryde was struck immediately by the comforting smells of beeswax and lemons – the smells of his childhood – and paused momentarily on the threshold. It struck him that Ryde

House, for the first time, felt mellow and welcoming. The floor tiles shone and the old table, polished and gleaming, had been moved to a more convenient location on the other side of the front door, where it had originally stood, many years ago.

The door to the drawing room stood open and he passed through. This room too bore witness to recent female invasion. The curtains had been pulled back and the spring sunshine poured into the room. A bright fire welcomed him and two chairs, cushions plumped, had been pulled forward to the fire, and waited invitingly. A bowl of ancient but still scented rose petals stood on the table. Best of all, the brandy tray had been placed well within reach of the chairs.

Lord Ryde poured himself a glass and wandered slowly around the room, examining its contents with sudden attention. Here was the small embroidery table his mother had used. And in here, because the library had been old Lord Ryde's particular domain, was the shelf where she kept her own favourite books. And in the corner, her footstool, old now, its red velvet sadly faded and worn, on which he had sat at her feet, listening as she read to him.

Returning to the fire and carefully standing with his back to the portrait of old Lord Ryde – which was certainly going to find its way to an attic before very much longer – he sipped the brandy and allowed his mind to wander back down the years. The welcoming warmth of the house after a long, cold day's shooting. Walking around the lake with his mother, looking for fish in the cool, dark depths. The contents of her needlework box scattered colourfully across the table. The sound of her voice in the hall, calling to Mrs Trent, the housekeeper of the time. He wondered vaguely what had happened to Mrs Trent. What had happened to all the servants of his youth? Pensioned off, he supposed. His father, whatever his faults, always acknowledged his obligations.

In contrast to his own behaviour. Even without

Bascombe's theft, he himself had always regarded the estate as nothing more than his own private bank – to be dipped into time and time again – to supply his demands, whatever the cost. And his demands had been heavy. What that opera dancer in Paris had cost him from beginning to end did not bear thinking about. Pouring himself another brandy, he wandered out into the hall and from there to his dining room. It struck him that the place was very quiet for the time of day. Completely silent, in fact, which suited his mood completely. He had no mind for small talk.

Again, the dining room smelled fresh and clean. Hours of elbow-grease must have gone into making the table's long surface gleam like that. How pleasant to come home from a hard day's work to warmth and comfort, a good meal and good company.

Home? What the devil had put that notion into his head. This was not his home. Had never been his home. Would never be his home. And as for what had put that notion into his head – that was easy. His lordship had no difficulty laying the blame on that white-faced witch upstairs, who flew at him every time he looked at her. Who defended the worthless George Bascombe with such passion. Who got herself shot, was now in his house and without even moving from her bed had disrupted his establishment with her women and their cooking and their cleaning – all against his express instructions – disrupting his life, undermining his clear intentions and God knows what else as well. Oh yes – he knew who was to blame for this current fit of blue devils as well. And to think she'd been here just twenty-four hours. Who knew what havoc she could wreak over the next few days?

His lordship resolved immediately to stay out of her way and to spend his efforts depleting the reserves of brandy from his cellar, thus rendering himself insensible – in every sense of the word – to any further outrages they – she – might perpetrate.

With this commendable intention, he strode back into the drawing room and slammed the door behind him.

Chapter Six

Alas for such good intentions. At eleven the next morning, two days later, his lordship was seated before the fire in the drawing room, brandy in hand and listening with misgivings to the sounds of mass disruption coming from the library. After spending some time mulling over the peculiar deafness of women, he had turned his attention again to the figures provided by his agent. These made disturbing reading and once he had rid himself of these blasted women, he would have Reynolds back up here again to explain himself.

He stretched his long legs before him, enjoying the knowledge that every female was safely somewhere else and not bothering him in any way at all, when the door opened, and leaning heavily on Miss Fairburn, her arm in a sling, Mrs Bascombe entered the room.

His lordship closed his eyes, briefly – an action not lost on either lady. Mrs Bascombe choked slightly. He stood uncertainly, and was deftly relieved of his brandy glass by Margaret, who had entered the room in Mrs Bascombe's wake.

Suggesting hopefully that Mrs Bascombe was not yet well enough to leave her room, his hopes were dashed when she informed him she had spent a peaceful night and was feeling very much better and, in fact, hoped she might be well enough to depart for Westfield the following day.

Lord Ryde, much to his astonishment, found himself saying nonsense, she must not attempt anything of the sort until the doctor had given his permission for such an enterprise, and it would have been hard to say who was most surprised to hear him say so. Pulling himself together, he

79

invited Mrs Bascombe to make herself comfortable on the sofa, ring for anything she needed and begged leave to depart, citing urgent business elsewhere.

Striding into the hall, he summoned the hapless Munch and demanded his horse be brought round immediately. Catching sight of a small, mob-capped female armed to the teeth with domestic implements, he gritted his teeth, essayed a smile and with the air of one getting to know the natives, said, 'Good morning, Eliza.'

'Good morning, my lord.' She bobbed a shy curtsey.

Silence fell. Both parties stared at each other across a widening sea of incomprehension.

'Settled in all right, Eliza?'

'Yes, thank you, my lord.'

Mr Martin approached.

'Good morning, Janet.'

She bobbed another curtsey.

'Eliza,' corrected his lordship.

'Er – no, sir. Janet.'

'You're sure?'

'Pretty much, sir, yes.'

His lordship turned to Janet.

'Janet?'

'Yes, my lord.'

'Not Eliza?'

'No, my lord.'

'Well, don't let me keep you.'

She dropped another curtsey that embraced them both impartially and disappeared.

His lordship watched her go.

'Wipe that smile off your face, Charles.'

'Yes, sir.'

'How the devil can you tell one from the other?

'Well,' said Mr Martin, accepting the question at face value. 'Margaret is tall. Janet is round, and Eliza makes wonderful pastry. It's easy.'

'Charles, you possess skills of which I can only dream.'

'Well, that's true enough. Hello, who's this?'

The front doorbell rattled.

A pause ensued, long enough for both gentlemen to realise that, having sent a message for his lordship's horse, Munch had obviously considered his domestic duties for the morning more than adequately discharged and had disappeared.

Eventually, Margaret appeared.

'Good morning,' said his lordship affably.

Behind her back, Mr Martin mouthed the word, 'Margaret'.

'I knew that,' said his lordship. 'Good morning, Margaret.'

'Good morning, my lord.'

She opened the door, stepped back, and announced, 'Lady Elliott, my lord.'

Possibly due to the cavernous nature of the hall, his lordship's faint groan was clearly audible.

Lady Elliott, a mother of five, three of whom were of the male sex and therefore had to have allowances made for them, could not help a smile.

To her surprise, this smile was returned by the graceless reprobate before her.

'Lady Elliott, how delightful. Again.'

'Lord Ryde, you make one so welcome I really cannot stay away.'

'So I had noticed, ma'am.'

She cast an appraising glance around the gleaming hall.

'I beg your pardon. I have come to the wrong establishment.'

'In that case, ma'am, do not let me detain you.'

She could not help laughing.

'Really, Lord Ryde, I do not know how it is, but I was never so rag-mannered before I met you.'

'Alas, ma'am, I hear that wherever I go. I can only

81

attribute it to my devilish good looks and debonair charm.'

She looked him up and down.

'Can you?'

It was his turn to laugh.

'Although it is delightful to see you again, ma'am, it must be Mrs Bascombe you have come to visit. You will find her in the drawing room. I am not sure how wise it was for her to leave her room so soon, but you shall judge for yourself. I hope very much you will remain for lunch and look forward to seeing you then.'

As Margaret led her away, he turned to Mr Martin, stating his clear intention to be off the premises before any more women turned up, and foreseeing that Miss Fairburn would be with Mrs Bascombe and Lady Elliott all morning, Mr Martin had no hesitation in joining him.

Returning some hours later, they were admitted by Munch who had resumed his duties and who advised them lunch would be served in twenty minutes. He frowned disapprovingly at their mud-spattered riding gear. Fortunately, both gentlemen were accustomed to fending for themselves, and speedily too, and were therefore able to join the party downstairs in time to escort the ladies to the dining room.

At least, reflected his lordship, he had nothing to blush for here. The room was stark and sparsely furnished – anything of even the smallest value having been long-since removed – but it was clean and polished and the table well laid.

And nothing to be ashamed of with the catering, either. The company enjoyed a light and elegant luncheon comprising two full courses, including a plate of honey cakes which more than captured Lady Elliott's attention. His lordship exerted himself and since he could be agreeable when he chose, kept Lady Elliott well entertained whilst further down the table, Mr Martin and Miss Fairburn chatted, shyly at first, but with increasing animation.

Mrs Bascombe ate a little, and then at Lady Elliott's urging, a little more.

'I regret, Mrs Bascombe, I have no fruit to offer you. Our succession houses are in a bad way.'

'Oh, no, my lord. The soup was delicious, but I will have one of those small cakes, if I may.'

Assuring himself that Lady Elliott was wholly engrossed in a three-cornered discussion with Mr Martin and Miss Fairburn over the relative merits of Bath over Harrogate, (to his certain knowledge, Charles had visited neither), he said in an undertone, 'Should you be up? If what I said has led you to believe I wish you gone, then I apologise most sincerely. You know, do you not, that you are welcome here for as long as you please?'

She held his gaze steadily.

'Yes, I do know that. I also know that if you do not stop making me so comfortable, my lord, I might never leave. This is in the nature of a holiday for me and I intend to make the most of it. You have been warned.'

'In that case, perhaps tomorrow, if you feel up to it, and weather permitting, you might like to stroll down to the lake with me. There is a little bench where you may rest and the views are very pretty.'

She smiled in delight and he thought the sun had come out.

'That would be delightful. I should love to.'

He reflected briefly on a woman whose existence had been so narrow that even a short walk was a major event. Unless, of course, it was his company she found so attractive. Watching her now, talking with Mr Martin and Miss Fairburn, he found the thought amusing.

He looked up to find Lady Elliott watching him closely and just for one moment, saw a hint of steel.

I know what you are about, said that look.

Lord Ryde experienced a spurt of anger that quite surprised him. That he could be suspected of harbouring intentions towards a woman, injured, a guest under his roof, after everything he had done to ensure her reputation remained intact was, he considered, more than insulting. He remembered again that he had not wanted to come to Ryde House, did not want to remain at Ryde House, could not wait to get away from Ryde House. And his small-minded neighbours.

He opened his mouth to utter a set-down that would send Lady Elliott out of the house as fast as she could move and probably Mrs Bascombe along with her and then caught Mr Martin staring at him, anxiously. He bit back what he had been going to say, telling himself that given his reputation, Lady Elliott's concerns were natural, remembered Charles' interest in Miss Fairburn, and that most importantly, he could not disappoint Mrs Bascombe.

He refilled Lady Elliott's glass himself, saying quietly, 'I understand your concerns, ma'am, but you may be easy. Perhaps sometimes we both forget it – but I am a Ryde.'

She had the grace to look a little ashamed and said in a low voice, 'I apologise, my lord, but you may have misunderstood me a little. She is so inexperienced and leads such a sheltered life … I do not accuse you, you understand, but it is very possible she might … misinterpret …'

'You need say no more,' he interrupted. 'But indeed, I think you worry unnecessarily. Both Mrs Bascombe and I seem to be incapable of holding any sort of conversation for longer than a few minutes without flying into a rage and abusing each other most soundly.'

At this point, Mrs Bascombe turned to Lady Elliot with some query and the conversation became general.

They lingered for some time at the table and consequently, the afternoon was quite far advanced when they made their way back to the drawing room. Lady Elliott, seeing the time, began to think of making her goodbyes, for no matter how grown up her children might be – Oliver was twenty-one, Clara nineteen, how time flies – she was a little nervous about leaving them to their own devices with Sir William not yet back from Rushford. The arrival of Margaret with the tea-tray, however, distracted her from these noble intentions and she sat back down again.

Mr Martin and Miss Fairburn seated themselves together with scarcely a break in their conversation. His lordship noticed sourly that the censorious Lady Elliott appeared to have no issues with this at all. He must obviously come to terms with the fact that his secretary was more socially desirable than he himself.

Lady Elliott seated herself comfortably and Lord Ryde hit on the happy idea of drawing Mrs Bascombe to the front windows and showing her the view across the grass to the tree-lined lake beyond.

Mrs Bascombe agreed that yes, it was very pretty and by standing on tip-toe and craning her neck she was just able to make out the little bench, installed by his mother, said Lord Ryde, because that particular spot had been a favourite of hers.

She was about to set down her cup and saucer when Mr Martin approached to relieve her of it. She was enquiring how long the walk around the lake would take when she heard a loud bang from outside, but quite close by. His lordship threw his arms around her and bore her to the floor as the glass in the window to her right shattered, showering her with broken glass and something embedded itself in the fortunately empty china cabinet on the far wall.

Mr Martin shouted a warning to Miss Fairburn, seized an astounded Lady Elliott, and pulled her to the floor, where she lay, too astonished to make any move and still clutching an unbroken honey cake.

Lord Ryde could not help reflecting that Charles's stock must surely now be as low as his own. Whatever his past sins, he had never actually manhandled a middle-aged lady to the ground. Actually, yes, he had. And this very day, too. He looked down at Mrs Bascombe, lying surprised but calm beneath him.

He said softly, 'Elinor, are you hurt at all?'

'No. You caught me very neatly.'

'Practice.' He raised his voice. 'Is everyone all right?'

'Yes,' said Miss Fairburn.

Lady Elliott remained silent.

'Lady Elliott,' said Mr Martin anxiously, 'Did I hurt you? Are you injured?'

Lady Elliott slowly became aware she was holding a honey cake and gently set it down on the carpet beside her.

'No,' she said, faintly. 'No, I am uninjured, thank you for asking. I really must enquire, however, just out of sheer curiosity, you understand, why Mr Martin suddenly took it into his head to hurl me to the floor.'

'Later,' said Lord Ryde, brusquely. 'Charles, come with me. Ladies, remain where you are, please. There may be further shots.'

'Take care,' whispered Mrs Bascombe, carefully brushing glass from his shoulder.

'I will.'

He touched her face with one finger, pulled himself to his feet and then he and Mr Martin were gone. They could hear male voices shouting instructions. Somewhere, someone, Mrs Munch probably, was having un-General like hysterics. The front door grated open and then the voices dwindled into the distance.

Margaret appeared in the doorway.

'Mrs Bascombe? Oh, my God, ma'am, what has happened?'

'Don't come in, Margaret. He may still be out there. Stay clear of the windows. And there is glass everywhere.'

'One moment, madam.' She walked gingerly around the edge of the room, picking her way through the broken glass and carefully drew the curtains.

'There, madam. Let me help you up.'

'No. See to Lady Elliott first, and then Miss Fairburn, if

you please. If no one minds, I'll just lie quietly for a while.'

Miss Fairburn's voice came from across the room.

'Elinor, my dear. Are you hurt?'

'No. Please do not be alarmed. I just have a tiny cut from the glass and my shoulder pains me where I fell on it. Please do not blame Lord Ryde. He could not help hurting me a little.'

'Of course not,' agreed Miss Fairburn. 'I'm sure he threw you to the ground as gently as he could. Stay where you are – I'll come to you.'

'No, Laura, pray do not. There is so much glass. Wait until the gentlemen return. Can anyone see what is happening?'

Margaret was peering through a chink in the curtains.

'I can see Lord Ryde, ma'am. And Mr Martin. They're in the trees by the lake. Mr Roberts is running around the back path. Mr Munch – oh, ma'am, he should not be running at his age. He has a cudgel. Mr Owen is coming along the path from the other direction. There is a lot of running and shouting but I don't think they have found anything.'

'Margaret, you must come away from the window at once,' said Miss Fairburn with authority. 'The assailant may still be concealed nearby. The gentlemen will be returning soon and Mrs Bascombe will require attention. Please go to the kitchen, do whatever is necessary to Mrs Munch, and return here with Tiller and bandages. Hurry, now. And keep everyone away from the windows.'

Margaret crunched away and Elinor, whose shoulder was throbbing most unpleasantly, closed her eyes and let the next ten minutes or so just wash over her.

She opened her eyes to find herself stretched on the sofa, with Miss Fairburn bending over her, and Lady Elliott clutching a bottle of smelling salts.

'Oh. Ugh. No,' she said, gently pushing her hand away.

'How are you feeling?'

'Surprisingly comfortable, all things considered.'

'Please remain still, the doctor is coming.'

'But why?' she demanded, struggling to sit up. 'I was not hit. Was I?'

'No, but ...'

'Oh, my Good, was someone else shot? Lord Ryde – is he hurt? Tell me at once.'

'No, no,' said Miss Fairburn, straight-faced. 'No one has incurred any injury at all. Apart from you, that is, my dear. You have started to bleed again and your hand is cut. Nothing to worry about, his lordship says, and the doctor will be here directly.'

'Did they find anyone? Did they catch him?'

'Elinor, please remain still. Here is Lord Ryde who will tell you himself. I must go now to Lady Elliott who is a little shaken.'

'Help me to sit up, first.'

She struggled to sit up and Miss Fairburn propped several cushions behind her.

Lady Elliott, also reclining on a matching sofa, was making occasional use of her own smelling salts.

All three ladies besieged Lord Ryde with questions.

'What did you see? Did you find him? What happened?'

Ignoring all this, he crossed straight to Elinor and dropped to one knee.

'Mrs Bascombe, how are you? Would you like me to help you back to our room?'

The thought of being banished to her room while exciting events took place without her was enough to bring the colour back to her cheeks with a rush.

'Certainly not, my lord. What do you take me for?'

'I take you for an invalid, ma'am, who has just sustained yet another injury. Do you know you are bleeding?

'It is just my hand, sir. Nothing to concern yourself over.'

'You must let me be the judge of that, ma'am.'

Mrs Bascombe, finding this not unpleasant, obediently lay back whilst his lordship examined what even he had to agree was a very minor wound and then carefully bound it up with his handkerchief.

Across the room, Miss Fairburn and Lady Elliott exchanged looks of astonishment.

When he had adjusted the bandage to his satisfaction, he rose and looked around him.

'Yes,' said Lady Elliott, acidly. 'We are both uninjured too, my lord.'

He seated himself alongside her.

'I am happy to hear it, ma'am. That such a thing should happen here is astonishing. I can only apologise.'

'Why? You did not order the attack. Did you?'

'Of course not. There are much easier and more reliable methods of ridding oneself of unwanted guests, ma'am. Not that I would ever dream of considering you such.' In a lower voice, he continued. 'You look very pale, Lady Elliott. Can I fetch Tiller? Or Margaret?'

Her lip trembled suddenly, but she managed a wobbly smile.

He put his hand briefly over her cold one. 'Shall I send for your carriage? Roberts and Owen can escort you home, though I doubt whether you will need them. Or I can send for Sir William. Just say the word.'

She sat up.

'Certainly not, my lord. If Elinor remains, as I know she will, then so shall I.'

'Bravo, ma'am,' said Miss Fairburn.

'In that case, Lady Elliott, may I offer you some wine?'

'You certainly may, my lord. And with all speed, too.'

'Shall we repair to the library? I think the ladies will be more comfortable there.'

'Yes,' said Elinor dryly. 'Not so many windows.'

Repairing to the library, they found the curtains drawn and candles lit.

'How delightfully sinister,' said Mrs Bascombe.

'It certainly lends a certain ambience to the room,' agreed

Lord Ryde.

'Yes, indeed,' said Lady Elliot, seating herself gratefully and accepting a glass of wine from Mr Martin. 'Who knows, by tomorrow, we may be under attack from all sorts of armed desperadoes and be forced to live under siege.'

'Oh, yes,' said Miss Fairburn, enthusiastically. 'We can hurl boiling oil on our attackers from the bedroom windows.'

'We should arm ourselves,' said Elinor with decision. 'Where is your gunroom, my lord?'

'I cannot remember,' said Lord Ryde, quickly.

'Never mind,' said Miss Fairburn. 'This is an old house. There will be pikes and halberds – and swords, too, I expect.'

'And armour. Do you have any armour? And …'

'No armour,' said his lordship with finality. 'No swords. No pikes. And above all – no guns.'

There was a short silence.

'It's very dull here, isn't it?' said Mrs Bascombe.

Chapter Seven

An hour later, some semblance of normality had been restored and Lady Elliott, now completely recovered after a reckless second glass of wine, had announced her intention, with Lord Ryde's permission, of course, of remaining at Ryde House that night and perhaps tomorrow, too. 'To support dear Elinor in this difficult time.'

Lord Ryde, visibly disturbed at the thought of yet another female polluting his bachelor establishment, nevertheless said everything that was proper and Roberts was despatched with an explanatory note and a request for her eldest daughter, Clara, to pack her overnight things.

Miss Clara had not, perhaps quite understand what was required of her, for several hours later, when the party was once again assembled in the library awaiting the announcement of dinner, a suitably dismal Munch made it known, in accents of doom, that another procession was approaching the house.

'Wonderful!' said Elinor. 'The enemy has mounted a cavalry attack. Munch! Bring caltrops and tripwire!'

Munch replied that he had brought wine, in a tone clearly indicating that this was all they would get, and that caltrops and tripwire, whatever they may be, would not be forthcoming.

Closer inspection, however, revealed the oncoming charge to consist of Lady Elliott's second carriage, containing Lady Elliott's luggage and Lady Elliott's maid.

'Another one,' muttered Lord Ryde to Mr Martin. 'At this rate, Charles, you and I will be sleeping on the roof.'

This conveyance was followed by the Westfield gig,

containing Porlock in all his awful splendour, together with such items Mrs Stokesley had deemed essential for Mrs Bascombe's continued well-being and comfort, to say nothing of that of Mr Porlock himself. The whole was headed by Sir William Elliott, on his Roman-nosed hack, in no good mood at having returned from Rushford and finding the wife of his bosom not only absent, but intending to remain so.

Dismounting, he tossed the reins to Munch, and with not so much as a glance at the chaos reigning behind him, requested a word with Lord Ryde immediately.

Lord Ryde, recognising the signs of a sorely tried man, took him at once to the drawing room where he could observe the scene of the crime for himself, plied him with wine and wisely did not attempt to interrupt his visitor until he had unburdened himself. It was apparent that it was the involvement of Lady Elliott that concerned him most. He was not mollified by Lord Ryde's cordial invitation to remove his wife whenever it suited him.

'It don't suit me at all,' said sir William, staring at him severely. 'There's something devilishly wrong here, my lord, and so, if you have no objections, instead of removing Lady Elliott,' (his lordship guessed she would refuse to go anyway, and this was Sir William's method of avoiding a distressing scene, in which he would have to exert an authority he was not sure he possessed), 'I propose to join you here.'

'You are very welcome, sir. I have made no complaint, but actually we are drowning in a sea of females here.'

Sir William gave a bark of laughter and threw him a shrewd look.

'Well, if that's the way you want to phrase things ...'

'It is. For the time being, anyway.'

'Hm. Well, a man don't get to our age without knowing his own business best, but there's something very wrong here, my lord. These attacks on Mrs Bascombe ...'

'Quite. I should warn you, however, that the ladies, far from succumbing to any feelings of alarm are, at this moment, planning to barricade the house, arm themselves to the teeth and repel all boarders. There has been talk of boiling oil.'

Sir William regarded him speechlessly for a moment, set his glass down with a snap and announced his intention of having a word with his wife immediately.

Lord Ryde, following him into the hall, became immediately aware that Domestic Strife had again fallen upon Ryde House. Munch and Porlock, those two ageing gladiators, stood chest to chest at the centre of a respectfully wide circle. It was obvious that Words Had Been Spoken. He was conscious of a craven urge to return to the relative safety of the drawing-room.

Porlock was enunciating.

'I have been summoned, Mr Munch, by Sir William Elliott himself, who has desired my presence to facilitate the daily running of the house.'

'Thought it wouldn't hurt to have another man inside,' muttered Sir William. 'No objection, I hope.'

'None at all.'

Munch drew himself up.

'That's as may be, Mr Porlock, but this is my house, and his lordship has always expressed himself as perfectly satisfied with my work.'

His lordship had absolutely no recollection of anything of the kind. Before he could intervene, however, Mrs Bascombe stepped forward.

Laying her hand on Munch's forearm, she requested a quiet word with him. They took themselves to a quiet corner.

Glancing over her shoulder, and speaking in a whisper, she said, 'The thing is, Munch, we ladies are naturally most upset by recent events, as I'm sure you can imagine.'

Munch nodded.

'We talked it over amongst ourselves and we agreed that

93

although we all felt perfectly safe under your care, this latest happening was just a little too close to home.'

Munch nodded.

'Well, Lady Elliott made the very excellent point that it wasn't fair to expect you to do everything – you know, run the house, supervise the servants, maintain our security …'

Munch nodded.

'So we had the idea of requesting Porlock, who, as we are both aware, Munch, is probably just kicking his heels at Westfield, while you are so overworked here …'

Munch nodded enthusiastic assent.

'So we thought to bring Porlock here to handle the day to day running of the household, whilst you, with your much greater knowledge of the house and its surroundings are now free to patrol and inspect and lock up and guard us and keep us all safe and secure. Oh, Munch, please say you will. We are relying so much upon you.'

His lordship, hidden in the shadows, listened to this shameless speech with huge appreciation.

Munch nodded importantly.

'You can rely on me, Mrs Bascombe.'

'Thank you so much. We ladies will sleep so much more soundly now. And I'm certain his lordship has some form of recompense in mind – you know, for all these extra duties.'

His lordship's appreciation vanished like the morning mist.

Mrs Bascombe met his look with a guileless smile and tripped back to join the others in the library.

Naturally, the second attack on Mrs Bascombe was the main topic of conversation at dinner. His lordship, presiding over a table laid for six, with a sideboard laden with dishes and both Porlock and Margaret serving, began to wonder if the dark cloud of respectability was descending upon him. Seeing his guests fully engaged in vigorous discussion and formulating plans to defend themselves, he smiled at Mrs Bascombe and asked if he should cut up her meat for her.

'Thank you, my lord, but I can manage.'

'I notice you are not wearing your sling.'

She twinkled at him, saying, 'Most inappropriate for formal wear, sir. If I had known you entertained so extensively, I would have packed accordingly.'

She was wearing a loose gown in her favourite shade of blue, tied under the bust with a matching sash – an informal outfit to be sure, but easy to put on and off and comfortable to wear. His lordship, an expert in women's apparel, approved.

'No matter, ma'am. You look quite charming.'

She was quite taken aback by this compliment, but managed to say, 'Thank you,' before her attention was claimed by Miss Fairburn. Encountering a Look from Lady Elliott, he smiled blandly and recommended she try another of her favourite damson tartlets.

'I still do not understand,' Miss Fairburn was saying for the third or fourth time, 'why Mrs Bascombe should be attacked. It's ludicrous. What possible motive could there be?'

'Well, ma'am, as I said before, if it is not Mrs Bascombe then the target was obviously Lord Ryde. He was present on both occasions.'

'Yes,' said Lady Elliott with unflattering swiftness. 'It is much more likely that someone would want to kill Lord Ryde.'

She met her husband's reproving glance and continued hurriedly, 'I mean – not that anyone would want to shoot you either, my lord – probably – it's just that of the two, you seem to be the more likely target.'

'I cannot disagree with you, ma'am,' he said, gravely. 'But even so, I am unable to think of anyone who would actually want me dead. Yes, I do owe money, but my creditors would certainly prefer me to live long enough to repay them. My heir loathes Ryde House and its surroundings even more than I do. And I haven't lived in

95

England for twenty years. I'm not worth much,' he concluded, and Elinor thought she detected a note of bitterness in his voice. 'But I'm certain I'm worth more alive than dead. So we're back to Mrs Bascombe again.'

Sir William's voice cut calmly through the storm of protest.

'Actually, my lord, no.'

The table fell silent.

Lady Elliott said uncertainly, 'My dear, what are you saying?'

Sir William laid down his knife and fork and looked around the table.

'I think you are, all of you, forgetting something.'

Silence.

Lord Ryde, who had more than once entertained this third possibility but refrained from mentioning it, waited to see what Sir William would say.

'You have discussed – very thoroughly indeed – the relative merits of Lord Ryde and Mrs Bascombe as the intended victim, but you all seem to have forgotten – on both occasions, a third person was present.'

Heads swivelled.

'Mr Martin? You were accompanying Lord Ryde in Green Lane and I believe you had just joined Lord Ryde and Mrs Bascombe at the window when the shot was fired.'

If there were doubts as to the attraction between Mr Martin and Miss Fairburn, there was now ample evidence for all to see. Miss Fairburn's eyes were large with alarm and fixed on Mr Martin who stared at her in consternation.

He pulled himself together.

'No, hang it,' he protested. 'Dash it all, sir, who would possibly want to kill me?'

'Where have I heard that before?' said Lord Ryde softly.

Lady Elliott was regarding Mr Martin with bright-eyed interest.

'Are you, perhaps, a lost heir?'

I'm a third son, ma'am. There are at least two lost heirs ahead of me.'

'Your father, perhaps ...'

'A clergyman. And himself a younger son. Believe me, ma'am, you'd have to decimate half Gloucestershire before my family would come close to inheriting anything.'

'Perhaps ...' said Mrs Bascombe. 'Are you perhaps in possession of some important knowledge and must be silenced before the truth comes out?'

Lord Ryde sipped his wine and wondered when dinner at Ryde House had become so entertaining.

'No, I am not, said Mr Martin, indignantly. 'At least I don't think I am. How would I know?'

'That's just the point, Charles,' said Lord Ryde. 'You wouldn't.'

'No, dash it all. I will not be murdered because I'm supposed to know something I don't know I know.'

'Well, you haven't, have you?' pointed out Mrs Bascombe. 'Been murdered, I mean. So far your shockingly inefficient assassin has only managed to hit me.'

'What a relief,' murmured Lord Ryde. 'So much trouble to find a new secretary, I mean,' he added hastily as Mrs Bascombe fixed him with an indignant glare.

'Especially one of my calibre,' said Mr Martin, modestly.

'Just so,' agreed his lordship.

Lady Elliott persisted. 'Are you perhaps in possession of a rich uncle?'

'Not in my family, alas.'

'A rich aunt then, who took a fancy to you when you were in your cradle.'

'Sadly, ma'am, my aunts are in possession of many qualities, but wealth is not one of them.'

'That is a shame.'

'I have often thought so, too.'

'Are you sure there is not some deep, dark secret, confided in you many years ago – by Lord Ryde, for example – and now you must be silenced?'

'I was standing next to him on both occasions,' objected Lord Ryde. 'Even if I was so muddle-headed as to go around blabbing my deep, dark secrets to all and sundry.'

'You have deep, dark secrets?' asked Elinor, wide-eyed over her wine glass.

'Yes. No. I believe we were discussing Charles as the probable target.'

No, my lord, I believe we had moved on to the far more interesting topic of deep, dark secrets,' said Mr Martin, helping himself to the damson tartlet Lady Elliott had, up to that moment, considered hers.

'I have none,' said his lordship, hastily.

The table stared at him in disbelief.

'Ahem! Prague!'

His lordship regarded his secretary.

'That's a nasty cough, Charles.'

'Indeed, my lord.'

'Could he, perhaps, have picked it up in – Prague?' asked Elinor, demurely.

Mr Martin smiled at her. 'I shouldn't be at all surprised, ma'am.'

Sir William called the meeting to order.

'It seems to me that on each occasion there were the same three people present and that none of them has any idea why they should be a target.'

'Perhaps we should split up,' said Mrs Bascombe, slowly. 'I could return to Westfield and see if the assailant follows me there. If I am shot again, you would then have a clear indication of how to proceed.

'Out of the question,' said Lady Elliott. 'You are not yet well enough to travel, my love.

'Oh, I don't know,' said Lord Ryde, thoughtfully. 'Am I alone in thinking Mrs Bascombe's murder could be quite helpful?'

'Yes,' said Mrs Bascombe, shortly.

'I think,' said Sir William, head of a large family and therefore skilled in maintaining focus, 'that we should continue as we are for the time being. Nothing can be done until Mrs Bascombe is recovered.'

'An excellent suggestion, sir.'

'My dear,' said Lady Elliot, 'I think it would be wise if you did not venture outside tomorrow until all this is over. There is no point in making things easy for him.'

Lord Ryde was watching the disappointment in Mrs Bascombe's face. 'Perhaps, ma'am, you would care to stroll around the walled garden instead. That would be perfectly safe and you could still enjoy the benefits of fresh air and exercise.'

Mrs Bascombe stared suspiciously at his lordship's carefully blank features.

'Thank you. That sounds very pleasant.'

The party broke up shortly afterwards. Sir William requested a word with his wife; Mr Martin took Miss Fairburn away to try her hand at billiards and Mrs Bascombe went thankfully to bed.

Chapter Eight

After her exciting day, Mrs Bascombe slept well into the next morning, arising, somewhat guiltily, just in time for lunch. She chose another very pretty gown in a soft blue and cream, taking a little more care over her appearance than normal.

Hearing that she was to venture outside, Tiller proffered a sunbonnet. Mrs Bascombe declined.

'Mrs Bascombe, ma'am' pleaded Tiller, nearly in tears.

'I will carry a parasol,' promised Elinor.

'But madam, you are not at home, now.'

Elinor suddenly realised that she had, in fact, been thinking of Ryde House as just that and pulled herself up short. Reluctantly, she took the bonnet. Tiller was privately of the opinion that she would probably spend the afternoon swinging the despised article by its ribbons as she walked bareheaded in the sun, before finally leaving it somewhere she could not remember.

After lunch, Lord Ryde escorted Mrs Bascombe to the walled wilderness at the rear of the building. Quiet and secluded behind high brick walls, the only sound was the hum of busy insects and the chatter of birds. Mrs Bascombe took a deep breath of pure enjoyment.

'Why won't you wear your bonnet?'

The happy moment vanished.

'I don't like things on my head.'

'Why not?'

Elinor groped for some suitable remark to turn the subject and failed. And now the silence had been too long.

'Why not?'

'I once sustained – an injury – to my head and find now that I do not care for headgear. Obviously, there are occasions when I must, but if at home, or if I count myself among friends, then I prefer not to.' She looked at him directly. 'Do I need to wear it now?'

'By no means,' he said, coolly, and taking it from her, threw it over the garden wall.

Elinor regarded him with rare approval.

'You didn't want it. I didn't want it. There seemed no point in keeping it,' explained his lordship. 'Tell me about your head injury.'

'No. How very sheltered is this garden. The sun is very warm here, is it not?'

'Yes. What happened to your head? Was it an accident?'

'No. What a shame the roses are not yet out.'

'Yes. Did you fall from your horse?'

'No. I would prefer not to discuss this any further. Shall we return to the house?'

'No. Tell me about the injury. Why are you so reluctant? Are you afraid?'

'No. What a splendid crop of dandelions. This must once have been a very pretty garden. I expect you remember that.'

'No. There is an old seat here. Shall we sit for a while?'

'No. Why do you avoid this house? Is it true you have not set foot here for twenty years?'

'Yes. Did someone cause your injury?'

'Yes. Do you hate this house that much?'

'Yes. Was it your husband?'

'Yes. As you well know. We will not discuss this. Have you always hated your father?'

'Yes. No. I … We …'

'Perhaps we should sit down, my lord?'

'One moment, please.'

He slipped off his coat and laid it on the bench for her.

'You didn't have to do that. The bench is quite dry.'

'You don't like wearing hats – I don't like wearing

coats.'

'Oh, no, don't spoil such a charming gesture. I was very impressed by your technique.'

He smiled a little sadly.

'My technique? I hardly think so.'

'Don't say that,' said Mrs Bascombe. 'This being probably the only opportunity I will ever have to have advances made to me by a confirmed rake, I was eager to see how you would begin. I have to say I am sadly disappointed so far, but that may be my own fault. Should I, perhaps, flirt a little as an incentive?'

He regarded her heavily.

'I really would rather you did not.'

She laughed. 'Oh, infamous of you to say such a thing! I am mortified.'

'No, Mrs Bascombe, you are changing the subject. Tell me about your husband.'

'Why do you want to know?'

'I want to understand.'

'But why?'

He drew a breath.

'I hardly know. But I do know that our two families are linked by the tragedy of That Night. It creates a bond. If we, of all people, cannot talk to each other about it, then who can we speak to?'

She was silent a long while.

He continued. 'I have never spoken of it – not even to Charles. Like you yourself, I suspect. Everyone knows – but no one talks about it. No one talks to *us*, Elinor. So, we have to talk to each other.'

She experienced a sudden and not-altogether-unwelcome urge to unburden herself; to share her thoughts with this hard-eyed, but not uncaring man. But old habits die hard. She took a deep breath but no words came. He sat beside her, unmoving in the morning sunshine. There was all the time in the world …

She fixed her eyes on a fresh bud, bursting with spring green. How long since her own spring? How much of her life had crept by without her noticing? Unbidden, her mouth opened and the words were found.

'He was drunk when he came home. It started almost at once. I tried to get out of the way. He caught me in the hall and just as things were getting really bad, Georgie came in. He did what he could, but he is – was – a very slight boy. He was no match for … You must understand this – Georgie never hesitated for a moment. His beating finished with a blow that knocked him sideways, and he was picked up, literally taken by the scruff of his neck and hurled out of the front door like an unwanted puppy. I don't know where the pistol came from, but the next minute, Ned was aiming at Georgie, still on the ground, only a matter of feet away. It would have been murder. I clung to his gun arm and shouted to George to go. To go now and not come back.

'He threw me across the hall – by my hair. I tumbled over and over. He seized me – by my hair again – and pulled me to my feet and did it again. He threw me against the wall. I could feel blood running down my face. He twisted his hands in my hair and shook me, left and right, like a terrier. He was shouting. Incoherently. I knew what he wanted. He wanted the money. Masters and I – we'd kept a small sum. We were keeping our creditors at bay with it. Promising first one, then the other. He mustn't have it or we would be finished. He was hysterical. It was fear. Everything was closing in. He was desperate. He would do anything. I couldn't get up. Porlock ran in. I heard shouting. He knocked Porlock down. Tilly – I don't know where she came from – was between him and me. She wouldn't move. He tried to pull her away. I heard the crack as he broke her arm. She screamed. Roberts came. With one of the gardeners. I was so frightened for them. I heard furniture being overturned. Tilly was still screaming but it was all such a long way off. Then there was another pain. I …'

103

She stopped.

A long, long silence ensued.

Lord Ryde was well aware that if he moved or so much as breathed loudly, she would bolt. He sat quietly, arms folded, leaning back against the warm wall, his eyes closed against the sun.

He gave her plenty of time and then said, in a voice devoid of any emotion whatsoever, 'And on leaving Westfield, Mr George Bascombe presumably fled straight to Ryde House.'

She responded with spirit.

'You know that he did.'

'I know that Sugden, my father's butler at the time, showed a dishevelled Mr Bascombe into the library at a very late hour. It must have taken him some time to get to Ryde House. The night was dark and he had no lantern. As Sugden told the story afterwards, my father was at his desk. Bascombe, breathless, shaking, and considerably bruised was given a brandy. Sugden was instructed to procure suitable clothing for the fugitive – as he was about to become – and left the room.

'When he returned with a top coat and hat and one or two other items, Bascombe was sitting by the fire, my father was sealing a letter and the safe door was slightly ajar. Sugden could not see the contents. He was dismissed. Some time later, he again entered the library to find my father unconscious on the floor and the safe wide open – and empty.

'No one knows what brought on the stroke – whether Bascombe actually attacked and robbed him, or whether it occurred naturally and Bascombe saw his opportunity, no one knows. They tried to question my father – and he was apparently desperately anxious to say something. Perhaps Bascombe had told him where he was going, left some clue – no one will ever know. He made every effort to speak – or write – but to no avail and eventually, the effort killed him.

'God knows, we had no love for each other, but the thought of him – he was a big man, you remember, vigorous and active right up until the end – the thought of him lying helpless of the floor, while that devil Bascombe plundered the safe before walking out as cool as a cucumber ... I tell you, Elinor, if I ever see George Bascombe again he will receive a taste of his own medicine – and more.

'I know ... I know you always look for another explanation. That you always fly to his defence. It is understandable – we all speak as we find. To you, he is a saviour, to me a thief and a murderer. We just don't know which. Maybe he is both. And since not one word has ever been heard from him since, I think it likely Mr Bascombe does not wish to be found. That he is in possession of a profitable estate and has never come forward to claim it, I think supports that assumption. Either that, or he is dead.'

He saw her close her eyes.

'I'm sorry. Does he still mean that much to you?'

'How can you ask? Did you not listen to what I told you? Without George Bascombe, I would be dead. It's all very fine for you, Lord Ryde – you are a powerful man – you could probably give a very good account of yourself under any circumstances, but I was helpless. George was half his size and he never hesitated – not for one moment. You have no idea – I still remember the feel of those cold tiles under my cheek, while he tried to kick the truth out of me in his rage. Ask Porlock who lay unconscious beside me. Ask Tilly whose arm will never work properly again. Ask them what sort of man my husband was and then ask them to tell you what George Bascombe did for me that night.'

She stopped, trembling uncontrollably, panting for breath while tears of anger and grief ran down her cheeks. With a huge effort, she drew a shuddering breath.

'I'm sorry, but I only know what I know. I've been told what he did that night at Ryde House, but I don't *know*. I wasn't there. But I was at Westfield and I do know what he did for me there. Therefore, that is what I believe. I believe what I know. You, my lord, were neither at Westfield, nor at Ryde House. You don't *know* anything. Only what you've been told. Because you weren't there.'

In one second, all his guilt and grief crystallised into a blinding, searing rage. That this woman who didn't even know him, could so unerringly put her finger on ...

Unheeding, he seized her arm. 'Are you saying this is my fault?' thus putting into words the terrible thought that had haunted him all these years. 'Are you saying if I had been here then this – none of this – would have happened?'

She held his gaze, tears still on her cheeks.

'No, my lord. You are saying it.'

He dropped her arm at once. She felt he had temporarily lost his place in the present and was looking back down the years.

It was her turn to sit motionless and wait.

Eventually, he said, 'This was not what I intended at all.'

'What did you intend?'

'I thought we could just discuss what happened, calmly and sensibly and perhaps something new might come to light.' He stopped. 'I never thought we would rip up at each other like this. We both have had our old wounds re-opened and to no good at all. I'm sorry.' He made a sad effort at a smile. 'Your words flicked me on the raw.' He stopped again.

She said, very quietly, 'You need not answer if you choose not to, but do you really think it was your fault. Because you weren't there?'

'Of course. How could it be otherwise? If I had been here ... If I had been here more, then George Bascombe might have been here less.'

'True,' she said. 'But when the events of that night occurred, he would still probably have fled here. It's closer than Sir William's house. And even if you lived here, you might not have been in that night – you might have been, but probably you would have been out, drinking, gaming, young women – you know the sort of thing.'

'*I* do,' he said grimly and with emphasis. 'But I am surprised – and appalled, ma'am – to hear that you do too.'

'Oh,' she said, innocently. 'They were my husband's chief occupations. I just assumed they were yours too.'

'Ma'am, I have many faults. I have done many things of which I am not proud. I expect, during the course of my useless life, to do many more, but please, do not compare me with your worthless husband, whose name, I notice, you can never bring yourself to say.'

She was silent for a while.

'No,' she said, eventually. 'You are nothing like him. Not at all.'

'I am very glad to hear that.'

'May I remind you, my lord, you were not here that night because your father himself sent you away and over the years he had plenty of opportunities to recall you and he did not avail himself of any of them. You were not here that night, but that was his fault, not yours.'

'I know. I know that, but sometimes, I think – could I have done more? Could I have made an effort to have been what he wanted me to be?'

'What did he want you to be?'

'Oh, sober, responsible, industrious, respectable, married … The list just goes on and on.'

'Another copy of himself?'

'Yes, if you like.'

'Oh no. He wouldn't have liked that at all. People never do, you know. They say, "Oh, you must meet Mr So and so. He's exactly like you and you have so much in common", and you end up hating them. I have frequently thought I would dislike myself very much if I ever met me.'

He couldn't help smiling to himself, but said, 'He wanted to be proud of me, I think.'

'Trust me, if he wasn't proud of his tall, handsome,

clever, popular, and charmingly irresponsibly son, who appears to me to epitomise everything anyone could want in an offspring – he certainly wasn't going to admire a sober, obedient, deadly dull, paler copy of himself. You would have irritated each other to death.'

He found himself unaccountably moved and to cover his emotion, turned to her. 'Handsome? Clever? Charming?'

'And tall. You forgot tall.'

'What makes you think that?'

'Well, that's what you are now, so it's hard to imagine that in your youth you were short, dumpy, stupid, and obnoxious.'

He laughed. For the first time in a very long while, it seemed.

'I wish I had known you years ago.'

'No, I suspect we would have disliked each other. I always believe there are paths to tread and lives to be lived before two people can be right for each other. Do not you?'

'Are we right for each other?'

'Oh, dear me,' she said, laughing in her turn. 'That wasn't what I meant at all. But I do notice you have not denied being short and stupid in your youth.'

'Well, I've never been short, but stupid …? Yes, I've managed that on an impressive number of occasions. I still do. Fortunately, I have Charles these days, and he has rescued me from the consequences of my stupidity on more than one occasion.'

'Yes,' she said, thoughtfully, 'Mr Martin. You don't really think he was the real target, do you?'

'No, of course not. I'm afraid we must accept, Mrs Bascombe, it's either you or me.'

'I think it's you,' said Mrs Bascombe.

'So do I,' he said, getting to his feet. 'Shall we walk a little more?'

He offered her his arm and they set off down another overgrown path. Mrs Bascombe's skirt, brushing the greenery, released spring scents into the warm air.

'Does that happen often?'

Deep in his own thoughts, he started. 'I'm sorry?'

'I asked, "Does that happen often?"'

Still baffled, he said, 'Does what happen often?'

'Having to be rescued from your own stupidity.'

'Rather more often than is appropriate for a – person – of my advanced years.

She could not see his face, but she could, again, hear a note of bitterness in his voice. She stopped, turned, and slapped his arm.

'Ow!' he said, in astonishment, stepping back. 'May I ask what I have done to deserve –?'

'More stupidity.' She cut across him. 'You were going to say "a gentleman" and changed it to "a person" because you don't feel you deserve the title. I don't know what you've done in the past, sir, but I do know that your behaviour to me (apart from the unfortunate episode when you threw yourself under my horse) has always been exemplary. You covered me when Archer appeared with his cart, for which I was exceedingly grateful. I know you held me while Dr Jacobs removed the bullet and that on another occasion, you were in my room making me drink something revolting and at no time have you ever spoken of it or made me feel uncomfortable in any way. You have borne the invasion of your house with fortitude and near silence, and as far as your limited resources allow, you have made us all as comfortable as you can. These, sir, are the marks of a true gentleman, not fine clothes or speeches, but consideration and an unobtrusive kindness, which you, my lord, possess in abundance, like it or not.'

He was too astonished to comment,

'And,' she swept on, 'do not speak to me of advanced years. Age has nothing to do with years. I know people – and you do too, I'm sure – who were born middle-aged. Who were old long before their time. Age is a state of mind and if you can only pull yourself from this – this Slough of Despond – into which you have, for some reason, plunged yourself, you, my lord, will be young until the day you die.'

If he had been astonished before, he was now completely bereft of speech.

Unfortunately, so was Mrs Bascombe. The silence lengthened.

Only too aware that not one, but probably half a dozen pairs of eyes were watching them from the house, his lordship again drew her arm through his and they resumed their walk.

'I shall say again, ma'am, that I only wish I had met you years ago.'

She was still to stricken to speak.

'You would have boxed my ears, Mrs Bascombe, and very likely those of my father as well, told us both not to be so damned silly and ...'

He became aware she was crying.

Fortunately, another seat was to hand.

'My dear madam – Elinor – please don't cry. Does your shoulder hurt you? Shall I fetch Miss Fairburn?'

She shook her head. 'No, no. I'm very sorry, my lord. I don't know why I am crying. I can assure you it was nothing you said or did. It just – happened.'

'And a very good thing, too. I suspect it is the combination of delayed shock and a difficult conversation. Please do not feel ashamed. I am actually quite relieved to see some tears. In my newly established character as a gentleman, please allow me to offer you a handkerchief.'

She took it and mopped her cheeks.

'I think,' he said, quietly, 'we should talk of other things. Let me change the subject. Tell me, ma'am, am I mistaken in thinking that Charles and Miss Fairburn are experiencing a definite – what's the word I want – attraction?'

She nodded, appreciating his efforts.

'I believe so,' she said, huskily. 'I cannot speak for Mr

110

Martin, of course, but even though Laura is usually very undemonstrative, I can see quite clearly that she seems to hold him in high regard. Should I be concerned? He seems a very pleasant young man.'

'He is. Intelligent and resourceful. He really deserves a higher position than I can offer him. It occurs to me that as well as ruining my own future, by taking him away from England all this time, I have also ruined his.'

'Please don't make me you hit me again.'

'I would be obliged if you did not. It does my dubious prestige no good at all for my household to see me being thrashed by a chit of a girl.'

'A girl?' she said, laughing.

'I believe my exact words were "a chit of a girl". You are not the only one in this garden who can deliver a few home truths, you know. You remind me of that princess who sits in the tower, waiting to be rescued.'

'What a ninny! Why doesn't she climb out of the window?'

'I have no idea,' he said in amusement, 'but the point I am labouring to make is that as a princess, she too is forever young.'

'I am very nearly as old as you, sir.'

'No, you are very nearly as *young* as I, ma'am.'

She snorted.

'That's better. Shall we continue our walk again? At this rate it will take us all afternoon to get around what is, actually, quite a small garden. Where were we?'

'Mr Martin and Miss Fairburn.'

'Yes, of course. I know nothing of Miss Fairburn. Charles, as we established last night, is the son – sorry, third son – of an impoverished cleric in Gloucestershire. I know nothing of Miss Fairburn's circumstances.'

'She is the oldest daughter in a large family. Her younger sisters are all married. One brother is in the army. The other is in the church. She is a loyal friend and I don't know what I would have done without her all these years. I'm afraid though, that although she has many excellent qualities, like Mr Martin, no one in her family is in a position to assist them. And ...' she broke off.

'You would miss her,' he finished for her.

'Well, I would. She came to me shortly after – shortly after my husband died – and apart from an occasional visit to her family, has hardly left my side. Selfishly, I would miss her enormously.

'Being in a similar position,' he said, 'I understand completely.'

'Yes, you do, don't you. And it would be so much worse for you. You have been together for so long. Would you continue your travels alone? Would you not miss your friend?'

He no longer felt any surprise that she was able to home in on his problems with such inevitable accuracy, and sighed.

'Like you, I would miss him enormously,' he said, surprised he could make this admission aloud. He had half-jokingly called her a witch, but was beginning to think he had been right, after all. 'And if they had even the smallest prospect of financial stability, I would not hesitate to promote the match, if that was what he wanted. It would be nice for at least one of us to have a reasonably normal life, but since there are no prospects for either of them, I wonder if it would not be kinder for me to invent some business and send him away before it becomes too serious.'

'I think that might be unwise. Mr Martin is not a green young man. Presumably he is not so blinded by love that he cannot see the problems ahead and if not, I know I have the greatest faith in Laura's good sense. Perhaps it will die a natural death and no harm done. I do not think you should risk alienating Mr Martin's allegiance by taking what might be unnecessary action.'

'I agree,' he said. 'That was my thought also, although I

confess my disinclination to interfere sprang from moral cowardice.'

'And what about you, my lord? With or without Mr Martin, what are your plans?'

There was no reply.

'Lord Ryde?'

'I don't know,' he said, eventually. 'My original plan was to collect my rents, sell what I could, take the money, and depart. I had not decided where to. Now there is this business with Charles, to say nothing of an apparent madman letting off shots whenever you are in the vicinity and my house is full of women.'

'Well, there is nothing to stop you placing your affairs in the hands of your agent and riding off to London to wait there until things are completed. Laura and I will be gone in a day or two and you can pretend none of this ever happened.'

'I could do so, yes.'

'So will you?'

'No.'

She let that lie for a moment.

'And where is your next port of call, sir? There cannot be much of Europe you have not seen. Will you venture further east, this time?'

Now for it. He took a deep breath. 'On the contrary, ma'am, I have actually been thinking of America.'

If she had been stricken before, she was truly paralysed now. Fortunately, he seemed not to notice her silence.

'Charles and I have talked of it, once or twice. The land of opportunity, you know.'

'What would you do there?'

'I'm not sure. Pursue whatever opportunities come my way, I suppose.'

'Forgive me, sir, but I have to ask. Are you running to? Or are you running from?'

He stopped dead.

'What?'

'It's a simple question. Are you running towards something or are you running from something?'

'I hardly see that it makes a difference.'

'On the contrary. Running towards something – a new start in a new land, for instance, is very different to running *from* something – Ryde House, your past, yourself even. If you are running from yourself, it hardly matters where you go, or even whether you go at all, does it? In the end, there is only one sure escape from oneself.'

And finally, she had insinuated herself right into his very deepest, darkest secret. What could he possibly say to her when he had no idea what to say to himself?

He turned on his heel and strode away. She heard the click of the gate and then she was alone in the garden.

Chapter Nine

Arriving back at the house, Mrs Bascombe was greeted by the news that his lordship had called for his horse, and gone out. Unable to meet Mr Martin's mildly enquiring look, she selected a book more or less at random from the library, and spent the remainder of the afternoon in her room, with the book open on her lap and not seeing a word.

Tiller took one look and forbore even to mention the sunbonnet, let alone ascertain its whereabouts. There was no sign of Miss Fairburn. Elinor came to the conclusion that her friend was old enough to know what she was doing and to stand back. Her friend might need her when Mr Martin departed.

By pretending to be asleep, she was able to avoid afternoon tea, but to refuse dinner would, she knew, cause more concern than was warranted, so she allowed Tiller to redress her hair and changed her light gown into something more appropriate. Taking her book with her as a shield against the world, she left her entrance into the library until very late and was thus able to avoid any private conversation with Lord Ryde, whom, she saw, had not bothered to change for dinner.

Responding to enquiries as to her afternoon, she was able to say, with only a tiny twinge of conscience, that she had enjoyed a very pleasant walk, thank you very much.

It would seem that Lord Ryde had also enjoyed a very pleasant walk and apart from a deepening of the lines around his mouth, and a disinclination to talk, he seemed very much as usual. Fortunately, Mr Martin and Miss Fairburn had plenty to say about their walk around the lake, and the fish they had spotted therein. This drew in Sir William, a keen fisherman, and by default, Lady Elliott also. Mrs Bascombe responded to any remark addressed to her, but initiated no conversation.

The ladies withdrew to the drawing room immediately after dinner, leaving the men to their wine. It struck Sir William that Lord Ryde was making even more free with the brandy than usual. They discussed fishing and shooting, and when they eventually joined the ladies, Mrs Bascombe, pleading fatigue, had already gone to bed. His remaining guests also retired almost immediately after the tea-tray had been brought in.

Left to himself, and very disinclined to seek his bedchamber, Lord Ryde instructed Porlock to take the decanter to the library and himself off to bed.

'Very good, my lord. Shall I shall light more candles in the library?'

'Don't bother. These few are more than adequate.'

'As you wish, my lord,' said Porlock, not betraying his thoughts by so much as a quiver. 'The house is locked up and I will leave your lordship's candle in the hall. Goodnight, my lord.'

Alone at last, his lordship kicked off his boots, threw his coat across a chair, stretched his long legs to the fire, and poured himself a generous measure of brandy to keep the dark at bay.

Upstairs, Mrs Bascombe had undressed slowly, climbed wearily into bed and reached for her book, only to remember she had left it downstairs. For some time, she lay and looked up at the ceiling and then abruptly sat up and reached for her dressing gown. The house was silent. She had heard everyone come up the stairs and disperse to their chambers. She could disturb Tilly, who would undoubtedly be in bed by now, or she could run downstairs, pick up her book, and be back in her chamber in under two minutes. Grasping her candle, she let herself out of her room.

116

The landing outside was by no means dark. A small oil lamp burned at the top of the stairs, showing the way. Another was set on a low table in the hall, rendering her own candle superfluous. Mrs Bascombe set hers alongside the oil lamp to collect on her return, and glided silently downstairs.

Entering the library, she flitted across the room like a small, white ghost and felt her heart leap from her chest as a shadow moved and revealed itself as Lord Ryde, sitting motionless beside a dying fire.

'What are you doing?' he demanded with all the exasperation of one who, for a fleeting moment, thinks he might have seen a ghost.

'It's me,' said Elinor, helpfully, if not grammatically.

'But what are you doing?'

'I left my book. What did you think I was doing?'

'How on earth should I know why you would take it into your head to wander around the house in the middle of the night?'

'Well, how was I to know you would be slumped by the fire working your way through an entire bottle of brandy?'

'You've known me for a week now. What the devil did you think I would be doing? Reading poetry? Come here.'

Mrs Bascombe, perceiving his lordship was three parts drunk, oddly felt quite reassured and fearlessly approached the fire. More embarrassed by her bare feet than actually being caught in her dressing gown, she curled herself up in the opposite chair. Tucking her dressing gown demurely around her ankles, she gazed at him expectantly.

His brief flash of anger had died away and he now found it hard to meet her disconcertingly bright-eyed gaze. However befuddled he might be, one thing was very clear to him.

'You shouldn't be here.'

'You told me come here,' she reminded him.

Not having a good answer to this, he picked up his glass, gazed in sudden revulsion at the contents and replaced it on

117

the tray at his elbow.

'Are you foxed?'

'I may be,' he admitted, cautiously.

She tutted.

'This is my house, my library, and my brandy, ma'am. Pray take your disapproval elsewhere.'

'You mistake me. It is not your drinking, but your inability to hold it that I am condemning. My father was right.'

Lord Ryde struggled a little to find his place in this wretched woman's conversation. Knowing he would regret it, he enquired, 'Your father?'

'Yes. I believe you knew him.'

'I knew *of* him.'

'Well, my father was always very loud in his condemnation of those who could not hold their drink. His proud boast was that he could outdrink not only the younger generation, whom he frequently stigmatised as cawkers, by the way, but most of his contemporaries like you, as well.'

'Like me?'

'Well, aren't you one of his contemporaries? After what you said today, you're obviously much nearer his age than mine.'

'I am forty-five, ma'am.'

'Good heavens.'

An ambiguous remark that might, at a push, convey admiration of his youth and vigour, but most probably did not.

'May I assist you in any way, my lord? Perhaps I can put another log on the fire for you. To save you bending down, you understand.'

At least now he recognised when she was being deliberately provocative.

'Go away,' he said, a trifle thickly. 'I need to finish the bottle and contemplate the ruin of my life and you are interfering with both. Go away.'

She glared at him. 'Now what have you done?'

'I beg your pardon?'

'You never mentioned your ruined life this afternoon, my lord, so I can only assume something catastrophic has occurred since then. What was it?'

Brandy loosened his tongue.

'It was you, Elinor. It's always you. You are the catastrophe that dogs my every waking moment. Dear God, I thought George Bascombe had dealt me a mortal blow, but you, with your mud-splattered face and above all, your damnable, infernal ability to pierce my very soul. And even now, at the bottom of a bottle, in the middle of the night, when a man might be safe, here you are, in my library and in my heart and I won't have you in either. Be dammed to you, madam, I wish I had never met you!'

He rested his head on the back of his chair and closed his eyes.

In every life there is a crossroads. A time when a decision must be made. A path must be chosen. Elinor sat quietly and a thousand disjointed thoughts flashed through her mind.

He was going to America. In one week he would be gone. For good. She would never see him again. It was unlikely she would ever leave Westfield and even more unlikely she would ever leave this neighbourhood. The spring and summer of her life were gone. She had never known passion. She probably never would. She had never been desired. Or known desire. Never wanted or been wanted to the edge of madness. Had Fate – or the devil – granted her one last chance? She could seize it. She should seize it. Was she really going to slide into indigent old age without just one golden memory to take with her? She was her own mistress. She answered to no one. And he was going away. And no one would ever know.

It seemed to her that her legs moved of their own volition. Hardly able to believe her own actions, she seated herself on the arm of his chair and put her arms around his neck, knowing that if he repulsed her now then she would die of shame. The sane half of her hoped he would. The other half remembered her sunbonnet sailing over the garden wall. Throwing her cap over the windmill …

He made a small sound and reached for her, pulling her down onto his lap. He took her hand and kissed her fingers.

'I can't do this. I can't take advantage of you like this.'

'On the contrary, my lord, it is I who am taking advantage of you.'

'I may be too drunk to know what I'm doing.'

'I am counting on it.'

'Elinor, you are a guest in my house. Dear God, when I think of what Lady Elliott would say should she walk in now.'

'Are you expecting her?'

'What? No, of course not.'

'Then why should she? Don't tell me you've been throwing out lures to her as well. She's a married woman. Have you no shame?'

'No. Stop. Stop. Elinor …'

'These protestations would be so much more believable if you were not holding me so tightly I can barely breathe.'

His grip slackened slightly.

'Don't you want me, my lord?'

He buried his face in her hair.

'God, yes. Beyond reason. Beyond sanity. I can feel your warmth and softness and I'm almost beyond control. You might as well be naked.'

'In a very short time, I hope to be.'

'Elinor, this is your last chance. For God's sake, go.'

'No,' she said softly. 'For your sake, I shall stay.'

He kissed her. Hard and fast, then released her, his eyes very bright.

'If you stay, you know what will happen?'

'I look forward to it.'

He stood, suddenly, lifting her with him and set her

gently on her feet.

She reached up and with trembling fingers, untied his already loosened cravat. His shirt came off over his head.

Still he held back.

'Elinor. Ellie, you are not the first woman I've had. Or even the tenth.'

'Oh, good. I look forward to being the recipient of your expertise.'

He swayed slightly.

'I have wasted so much of my life.'

'You are lucky. My life was wasted for me. Please. Ruin me. Ruin me now.'

His mouth came down hard and he pushed himself against her, all caution gone. She reached eagerly for him. Somehow, her dressing gown came off and pooled around her ankles. He wondered briefly if she trembled with excitement or fear. He was on fire for her, his blood thickening. Desire had become a need. And that need had become an imperative. If she touched him now …

Again, he drew back.

'I can't. Oh God, Elinor. This should be a special time for you. I know you've been married before, but I should make this wonderful and all I know is that I want you. Now. Hard. I am so insane with desire for you that I can't give you what you deserve and …'

'Never mind what I deserve. Give me what I want.'

She untied the ribbons of her nightdress and pulled it down over her shoulders. It slipped to the floor with the faintest whisper of silk and it was his undoing.

He bore her backwards, remembering her injured shoulder just in time to cushion her fall. Her hands scrabbled at his waist. He tore at his breeches and kicked them away. Her body was a miracle of shadow and light and he gave himself up to it. Lost in her. Drowning in her.

For Mrs Bascombe, it was a revelation. Similar occasions in the past had been an opportunity to review the crop

121

timetable or calculate the rent roll for the coming quarter. She now found herself unable to remember her own name, far less catalogue the repairs necessary to the old barn.

His hands were rough and demanding. There was no gentleness in him. Nor did she want it. She wanted to explore him. To touch every inch of him. To curl her fingers in his coarse chest hair. To run her hands over his flat stomach. To feel his muscles clench. To hold him. To stroke him. To push him past all control …

He was whispering incoherently into her hair. His breath was hot on her neck. His hands were everywhere on her body at once. She was lost – in every sense of the word; her heart thumping so loudly he must surely be able to hear it. He could certainly feel it, as she could feel his. Beating fast and hard. Racing.

Heat pooled low in her belly and when he touched her there, her legs moved of their own accord. His fingers moved inside her and she cried aloud, a storm of sensation breaking over her. She could feel a rhythm. Tension built inside her, demanding release – violent release.

They were equal in their need for each other. Two lonely people, whose lives had been blighted and had never recovered. He – going to the devil as fast as he could manage and she just wishing she could. No longer satisfied by his life, he needed to come home. She – no longer satisfied with her life, needed to escape. To spread her wings. To fly.

And then he was pushing himself inside her, matching her rhythm, matching her breathing, moving with hard, strong thrusts, giving and receiving pleasure, while she arched herself towards him, clawing at his back in her own frenzy, soaring, until suddenly, the world fell away. There was silence. And falling. And deep happiness. And again. And again. Until finally, there was nothing left.

She opened her eyes. He had moved slightly, his weight was lessened and she could catch her breath. One hand still cupped her breast. And he was crying. Quietly. She could feel his body shudder. She closed her eyes and let pity overwhelm her.

When she opened her eyes again, he was sitting beside her, wearing his shirt. He had covered her with her dressing gown. She should not, she knew, draw comparisons between this and previous experiences, but this little courtesy surprised and moved her.

'Thank you, my lord.'

'Elinor, we have just given ourselves to each other. I think you may now use my given name.'

'John.'

'Why do you say that? Most people call me Jack. Only my father called me John.'

'Jack is another man. John is the man here today. I prefer John to Jack.'

'I think – so do I.'

He lay down beside her.

'I love having you here beside me. I would give anything to sleep now and wake tomorrow with you still here. But at the risk of sounding discourteous, my little witch, you must go.'

'I am impressed at this concern for my shattered reputation.'

'As you said, Jack is gone. It is John Ryde speaking now and he is in a fever of anxiety that someone will walk in. There would be hell to pay, you know. Neither of us would survive.'

'I do know. I thank you for your care of me. Again.'

He drew her to her feet.

'Let me help you.'

'You?'

'Well, I admit I am more accustomed to removing female apparel than replacing it, but it seems fairly straightforward. One simply reverses the process.'

Two tangled minutes later, he was forced to admit defeat.

'Stop laughing, Elinor.'

123

'Your efforts are commendable, but you definitely need more practice.'

'It's not easy, you know. There are only so many times you can forcibly dress a woman.'

'Should I send Tiller to give you some lessons?'

'I am not dressing and undressing Tiller, Elinor. Not even for you.'

'I am ready now. You may, if you wish, salvage your self-respect by tying my sash.'

'And now, I shall escort you to your room.'

'Thus ensuring, that should we be seen, everyone will know what has been happening. I will go alone and if anyone sees me, I have been collecting my book. Goodnight … John.'

He cupped her face in his hands.

'Tomorrow, I want to talk to you. In the meantime, goodnight, Ellie.'

The oil lamps were still burning. The house was still silent and she found her candle with no difficulty. Congratulating herself that no one would ever be any the wiser, she slipped quietly into her room to find Laura Fairburn awaiting her.

Mrs Bascombe softly closed the door behind her.

They contemplated each other.

'Laura, they're going to America.'

Miss Fairburn paled.

'Both of them?'

'I don't know.'

'Elinor, they can't. What can we do?'

Mrs Bascombe smiled slightly.

'Well, I have made a start.'

Mrs Fairburn got to her feet with sudden decision.

'Then so can I!'

Mrs Bascombe had a sudden vision of her friend marching down the landing, fired with resolve – and possibly other things – while Mr Martin slept peacefully on, unaware of his fate bearing down upon him..

She put out a hand,

'No, Laura. No. '

'But Elinor …'

'No, Laura. I have been married. I'm a widow. I answer to no one. You, on the other hand …'

'It doesn't matter. If I never marry then it's not important.'

'Oh, Laura, it does matter. You know it matters. Our cases are not the same. And your Mr Martin is an honourable man.' As opposed to Lord Ryde, who most definitely was not. 'Do not, I beg of you, put him in that position.'

'But America?'

'They are not there yet. Do not despair. Something may yet happen.' She took her friend's hand. 'We have fixed worse things than this, Laura. Just promise me …'

Miss Fairburn smiled. 'I promise. And now, with second thoughts, I'm sure I would have run away before he opened the door.'

She stood up.

'I'm tired and I'm sure you must be, too.'

'A little. Why are you here, anyway?'

'Oh, I thought I heard a sound. I wasn't sure if it was inside or outside. I came to see if you heard it, too. But you weren't here.'

'I went to get my book,' said Mrs Bascombe, firmly.

'And where is it?'

'Oh.'

'Oh?'

Mrs Bascombe gave up. It had been a long day.

'We will talk about this tomorrow,' and remembered Lord Ryde saying something very similar. It was going to be a long day tomorrow, as well.

Chapter Ten

If Mrs Bascombe thought meeting Lord Ryde over the breakfast table the next morning would prove awkward, she was mistaken. He barely glanced up as she entered the room, greeted her politely but casually, and resumed his conversation with Sir William. They were discussing fishing again, she gathered.

Mrs Bascombe had a busy breakfast. She received the news of Dr Joseph's impending visit with equanimity, she debated the merits of rod over line with Sir William, a subject about which she cheerfully admitted complete ignorance and agreed demurely to another walk in the walled garden with Lord Ryde, should the weather stay fine.

Dr Joseph professed himself delighted with his patient but warned her against attempting to do too much too soon.

'For I know you of old, Mrs Bascombe and I hope very much this will be my last visit. Your wound is healing exactly as it should and provided you behave yourself, I foresee no problems at all. Miss Fairburn, I rely upon you.'

So saying, he closed his bag, informed Mrs Bascombe she should be well enough to return to Westfield the next day, or possibly the day after – which was something Mrs Bascombe unaccountably forgot to mention when she joined Lord Ryde in the walled garden later that morning.

The day was cooler than yesterday and Mrs Bascombe wore a high-necked gown and her favourite Paisley shawl. They walked a little way and then, at his lordship's suggestion, seated themselves, out of the wind.

'How are you this morning?'

'Very well, thank you, my lord.'

126

'I thought we had agreed you would use my name.'

'Only when we are alone.'

He looked round in amusement.

'Elinor, we are alone.'

'Very well … John.'

Extraordinary, she thought, considering her shamelessness of last night that she should feel so shy using his name.

'What did the doctor say?'

'That everything is healing just as it should and not to do anything foolish.'

'Really? How long has he known you?'

She smiled and cast around for a safe topic of conversation.

'So what are your plans, my lord? You will be so pleased to see the back of us, I think. Do you intend to visit London, at all?

'My plans are – uncertain – at this moment.'

'Are the rents not coming in as quickly as you would like?'

'Nothing is going as I would like.'

She waited for more but he remained silent and she was forced to ask, 'In what way?'

'The money is not coming in. Two of my tenants have disappeared. For good, I suspect. My house is full of memories. And women. I have been shot at – twice. I have been forced to leap for my life and my heart was stolen while I wasn't looking.'

'Two of your tenants absconded?' said Mrs Bascombe, ignoring the rest of this speech and her suddenly accelerated heart rate. 'That is very bad news. Did they take much?'

'Everything that wasn't nailed down, I believe. But that is not the point.'

'No, you can always find new tenants. May I recommend …?'

'No, Elinor, you may not!'

127

Silence fell.

'Are you going to brood?'

'What?'

'Are you going to brood? I believe that is the accepted form of behaviour for the badly dressed, melancholy hero who broods on dark disappointments, previous crimes, and nameless passions as he stalks his desolate acres. I've never seen anyone brood before. Do you mind if I watch?'

'Is that how you see me?'

'Indeed. You fit the bill exactly. You're melancholy – well, a little sulky, actually, but close enough, and you yourself have admitted to any number of nameless passions. Why, only last night, you said …'

'Yes, never mind that now,' he said quickly. 'I do not brood. I am not sulky, although given the provocation, it's a miracle that I am not. And I certainly do not stalk my desolate acres.'

'Yes, you do. The first time we met you were contemplating a ditch. I believe this to be quite common behaviour for heroes. And I note you have not denied the badly-dressed charge. Like it or not, my lord, with your behaviour, your surroundings, your appearance – you are every young maiden's idea of the romantic hero.'

'Mrs Bascombe, I no longer find myself amazed that you have been shot. My astonishment is now that you have only been shot once!'

She went into peals of laughter and after a while, so did he. She watched him lean back against the wall, still smiling. It struck her that even though there might be more women and fewer tenants in his life than he would have liked, he looked far more relaxed and less unhappy than he had a week ago. Some of the harsher lines around his mouth had smoothed away and the laughter lines around his eyes were more pronounced.

'That's better,' she said, approvingly. 'Nothing is ever as bad as you think. Your agent will find you new tenants easily enough. The rents will come in. I shall be gone soon and my entourage with me. Ryde House will sink back into dust and decay and the only trace of our passing will be the ghostly echo of our voices in the halls. It will be as if none of this ever happened.'

Apparently carelessly, she played with the fringe of her shawl and no one would have guessed her heart was beating so fast as to make her feel sick.

The long silence made her look up. He was staring down at his feet.

'Have you thought any more about America, sir?'

'No.'

This uncompromising reply left her slightly at a loss and in the silence, he turned to her.

'What are your plans, Mrs Bascombe?'

'Well, when I leave here for Westfield ...'

'No, not that. I mean, if you could choose your future, what would you choose?'

She was, as always, a little bewildered, since throughout her life she had had very little experience of being allowed to choose for herself.

Discarding her first reply as completely inappropriate, she said, 'Well, Laura and I have always thought we would like to spend a few weeks in Bath.'

'Bath?'

'There is no need to sound quite so thunderstruck. It is, I believe, a very pleasant place.'

'I daresay, but as a life's ambition, just a little – well – small.'

She never knew whence came that sudden spurt of anger.

'I expect is seems that way to you, my lord. You, who can go where and whenever you please. I, on the other hand, am forced to cut my cloth to suit my purse. Mine has been a small life, but my expectations, while they are correspondingly small, mean a great deal to me. Good morning.'

129

It would have been an excellent exit line had she actually been allowed to exit. He prevented her leaving by simply grasping a fold of her dress and pulling her back down again.

She subsided into resentful silence.

'I did not mean to offend you,' he said, mildly.

'Then I congratulate you on your performance. You have achieved maximum effect with minimum effort.'

'What a shrew you are,' he remarked amiably.

'I freely admit that I have sometimes provoked you, my lord. Deliberately, too. But I never thought you so mean-spirited as to hold me in contempt simply because, unlike you, my sex and circumstances prevent me achieving your giddy heights.'

He jerked back as if she had slapped him.

'What?'

She swept on.

'Look at you – born with every advantage the world can offer. Birth, breeding, fortune – and what do you do with it? Squander it all away on momentary gratification and sulk when there's nothing left. And did it make you happy?'

'Is this any of your business, madam?'

'Let us just say that it made you what you are today. There – I think that answers your question in a way that even you will understand.'

Lord Ryde, who had meant to avail himself of the opportunity to ask a very different question, could only thank Providence for its merciful intervention. All the old dislike for the place, rooted in years of resentment and a sense of betrayal came flooding back. He shuddered inwardly to think what a narrow escape he had had. That a few days of comfort, good cooking, and a pleasant companion could so undermine his resolve to be gone was unnerving. He had no hesitation in laying blame at the correct door and took refuge in frigid courtesy.

'Indeed, ma'am. I thank you for your opinion – refreshingly vigorously expressed – if unasked for.

Perhaps …'

But at that moment, the gate clicked open and Porlock was before them, bearing a calling card upon a silver salver.

'I beg your pardon, my lord, madam. A visitor has called.'

'A visitor?' echoed Lord Ryde in astonishment. 'For whom?'

'I believe, my lord, it is Mrs Bascombe whom they wish to see, but they asked for you, as well.'

Mrs Bascombe looked at his lordship who shrugged. 'Don't look at me. Almost everyone I know in England is already here.'

Porlock proffered the tray and Mrs Bascombe picked up the card and read aloud, 'Major Lionel Pirie. The name means nothing to me.'

'Nor I. Is he alone?'

'No, my lord, he is accompanied by a lady. Possibly his sister, from some remark I overheard.'

Mrs Bascombe's eyes danced.

'A young lady – accompanied by her brother? I think we can guess what this is about.'

Porlock coughed, thus signifying disapproval at this levity.

'Oh no, madam. A most respectable couple. Very pleasant, if I may say so. I should perhaps mention, my lord, madam, they are in mourning.'

'A mystery,' remarked Lord Ryde getting to his feet. 'Are you well enough to receive visitors, Mrs Bascombe, or shall I see them on your behalf?'

Mrs Bascombe did not dignify this with a response.

Entering the drawing room just ahead of Lord Ryde, she saw two people standing near the fire, warming their hands and apparently examining the late Lord Ryde's portrait hanging over the mantel.

She saw a couple, both probably in their early thirties, dressed, as Porlock had reported, in mourning. The gentleman, sporting magnificent whiskers, had the unmistakeable air of a military man. He advanced now and bowing to Mrs Bascombe, enquired, 'Mrs Bascombe? My name is Pirie and this is my sister … er … Catherine.'

His voice was quiet and he seemed slightly ill at ease.

Still slightly bewildered, Mrs Bascombe murmured a greeting. 'Good morning, sir, Miss Pirie.'

He hesitated and cast a glance at his sister. 'No, not Miss Pirie, ma'am. My sister is – was – married.'

Some instinct made Lord Ryde stroll forward and introduce himself, taking care to station himself close to Mrs Bascombe.

'How do you do, my lord. We are both extremely sorry to call on you uninvited. I hope we are not inconveniencing you. We considered writing ahead to Mrs Bascombe, but this is a very personal and private matter and we decided it would be easier for all concerned if we called in person.'

Mrs Bascombe still looked baffled. Almost certain he knew what was to follow, Lord Ryde took the opportunity to invite his guests to be seated.

They did so and a short silence fell. Finally, the Major took a deep breath, turned slightly to face Elinor and said, 'I beg your pardon, ma'am, but when I mentioned my sister … That is … No, this will not do. There is no other way to say this. Ma'am, please allow me to introduce my sister – Mrs George Bascombe.'

Long moments passed. Lord Ryde, with some concern, awaited the moment Mrs Bascombe would take in the full implications of this visit.

She seemed bewildered. 'You – you are George's wife?'

'Yes,' said the lady, speaking for the first time. Her voice was soft and low. She seemed on the verge of tears and those tears were not for herself. 'We were married nearly four years ago. In India. Calcutta.'

She paused.

Elinor had gone dreadfully pale.

'You are not married now?'

Lord Ryde guessed she could not bring herself actually to ask if George was dead.

Major Pirie said gently, 'You see now that this was not news to be conveyed by a cold letter, or through your man of business. My sister tells me George spoke often of you, ma'am. He held you in considerable affection. We are anxious not to cause you undue distress. Mrs Bascombe, I am very sorry to inform you that Mr George Bascombe is dead.'

Mrs Bascombe had the strangest sensation that the ground had opened beneath her feet and plunged her into a pit of icy cold water. Sound receded. She could see mouths opening and closing as the others talked on.

George. Gone forever. She had always known this day would come. She had had years to prepare for it and now it was here at last and the news caught her a blow over the heart that stopped all the breath in her body.

The other Mrs Bascombe talked on. And on. George in Calcutta. George at work. Handsome George. Popular George. But all she saw was George sprawled on the floor. Ned standing over him, his face flushed with drink and rage. Grabbing George by the scruff of his neck and pitching him contemptuously out of the door. George, white-faced with shame and fury, struggling helplessly. To be pitched headlong from his own home into the night. George who would have plunged straight back in again – overwhelmed and undersized but with a heart as big as a lion. George who was so loth to leave her and only when the gun went off and she screamed at him to run – to run and never come back – had he fled into the night. Having done what he could. Only then had he left her. And now he was dead. George was dead. Her champion. George was dead.

Mrs Bascombe's face was frozen and white. She made no move or sound. Even Lord Ryde himself hardly knew how he felt. Shock, certainly. Some distress on Elinor's

133

behalf as well. Disappointment at being denied the satisfaction of revenge. Now he would never know what happened that night. Never know how he did it. What he did with the money. He would never have justice for his father now.

Reasonably certain that none of this showed in his face, he stood up and rang for Porlock, who entered with refreshments.

Mrs George Bascombe gratefully accepted a cup of tea. The gentlemen took a glass of wine. After one look at his mistress, Porlock poured a very little brandy into a glass and handed it to her with a gentle murmur.

Major Pirie was speaking.

'I – we – are so sorry to bring you such sad news, Mrs Bascombe. We thought it right to see you as quickly as possible and have posted directly here with all haste.'

Lord Ryde suspected they had also taken this opportunity to inspect their newly acquired property, Westfield. But then, they would hardly be human if they had not succumbed to a little curiosity.

Major Pirie carried on.

'You must not think, ma'am, that this will make any difference to your current circumstances. Please allow me to speak freely. My sister and I are very well aware of the condition of the estate left by your late husband, and of the enormous task you undertook to set it on its feet again. That there is anything worth inheriting is due entirely to your efforts, ma'am. We are very grateful.'

'Inheriting?' Lord Ryde looked up sharply.

Mrs George Bascombe set down her cup and turned eagerly to Elinor.

'I have a son. George's boy. He's nearly three now and such a bonny boy. I do hope you will love him, ma'am. He is so like his father. Every day …' she broke off and groped for her handkerchief.

Porlock murmured again and obediently, Elinor took a sip

of her brandy.

It was Lord Ryde, who, after a glance at Elinor, asked. 'Are you able to tell us how Mr Bascombe died?'

Since Mrs George Bascombe seemed unable to answer this question, again, Major Pirie took up the tale.

'The tragedy is, ma'am, that George was actually on his way home back to England. Little Georgie's birth made him very aware of his roots. He felt very strongly that his son should know his home – and you too, ma'am. He sold everything he owned and booked passage for himself and his family on the *Athena*, calling in at Cape Town.'

'You did not travel with them,' asked Lord Ryde.

'I was in Cape Town with my regiment, the 72nd,' replied the Major. 'I was to meet the boat and spend a few days there with my new family.'

He drew a deep breath.

'When the ship docked at Cape Town, I was waiting on the quay. I had not seen my sister for some years – and her husband and son not at all. You may imagine my anticipation. However, when the ship docked, Mr Bascombe was dead. He had succumbed to some shipboard malady. It was all over very quickly. He died, apparently, with Cape Town actually on the horizon. My sister was distraught, as you can imagine. The captain, a very decent man, assisted with the formalities and George was buried in the European cemetery there. Quite a pleasant spot, ma'am, if that offers you any consolation.

'I could hardly leave my sister to continue the voyage alone and there was nothing for her to return to Calcutta for, and so, with my commanding officer's permission, I have escorted them to England.'

'And where is Master Bascombe at this moment?'

Mrs George Bascombe smiled. 'With my family in London, being thoroughly spoiled by aunts, uncles, cousins, servants, and anyone else he can induce to give him what he wants.'

135

'He sounds very like his father,' commented Lord Ryde and thought Mrs Bascombe must indeed be in a bad way that she did not immediately rise up in wrath and smite him with the tea pot.

Neither the Major nor Mrs George Bascombe appeared to be aware of the true nature of this remark and happily took it at face value.

'He is,' said Mrs George Bascombe, fondly. 'He is the most loveable little man. Everyone who meets him falls under his spell. I would have loved you to have met him, Mrs Bascombe, but after such a long voyage, it seemed best for him to rest a while. And since we plan to return to London with all speed, reluctantly, I left him behind.'

'You do not plan a long stay here, then?' asked Lord Ryde.

'No,' replied the Major. 'My sister is anxious to return to her son. I am planning to sell out, with everything that entails and there are relatives to visit – hundreds of them, apparently – to show off little Georgie and a million other things to do before we can even think of moving to Westfield.

'Which brings me to what I was saying, earlier, Mrs Bascombe. My sister and I hope very much that you will not regard our arrival as any sort of reason to quit the place. Firstly, it is your home and we hope very much that it will continue to be so. We do not expect to return for about a twelvemonth and we would be so grateful if you could remain at Westfield until then and long beyond as well. I'm a military man, ma'am, always have been, and land management is a mystery to me. My greatest fear is that you will abandon us to our ignorance. Obviously, you may take an instant dislike to us and not wish to stay on, in which case, you may rely on us to make everything as easy for you as may be. It shall all be exactly as you choose, ma'am. We are all aware that without you, there would be no Westfield. Whether you go or stay shall be your choice, but we both hope you will stay. And we are confident that once you clap eyes on little Georgie you will want to do so.

'And now, this has been a difficult interview for all concerned. I can see, ma'am that you are still deeply shocked. My other reason for calling was to ascertain the name and address of your man of business, who resides, I believe, in London, so that I may call on him with all the papers and documents he will demand.'

'I believe I shall be able to provide these details, sir,' murmured Porlock.

'Thank you. I shall leave our London address with you, should Mrs Bascombe wish to contact us at all. I expect when she is a little recovered, she will have many questions.'

Porlock bowed.

Mrs George Bascombe rose to take her leave. Casting a worried glance at Mrs Bascombe, who, although she had automatically risen with everyone else, was plainly not thinking clearly, she put out her hand, saying in her pretty voice, 'I am so sorry, Mrs Bascombe. This has been such a shock for you. We will leave you in peace now, but I do hope I may write to you. I have never had a sister before and have very much looked forward to making your acquaintance.'

Mrs Bascombe blindly shook her hand. Major Pirie Bowed and Porlock ushered them from the room. Lord Ryde followed them out. The door closed behind them.

While Porlock disappeared to fetch the promised information, Major Pirie expressed his concern for Mrs Bascombe.

'This has been a difficult time for her,' said Lord Ryde. 'She sustained an accident a few days ago that has confined her to this house. As no doubt they told you at Westfield'

'Oh no, we did not call in. My sister felt we should not push ourselves forward. Especially since we do not expect to return for a long while.'

'I think, when Mrs Bascombe is recovered a little, she

will appreciate such thoughtfulness.'

'I hope the accident was not too serious. Today's news will not have helped.'

'No, indeed. I believe this is your carriage.'

The mud-splashed conveyance pulling up outside the door was undoubtedly hired, but of good quality. The Major was obviously a man of means.

'A cut above your average hired team,' said Lord Ryde. 'From the Red Lion in Rushford?'

'No, we came directly from Hereford.'

'Will you return there tonight?'

'We are not sure. My sister tires easily. Kitty, are you ready?'

Porlock approached and proffered a piece of paper.

'You should find everything you need there, sir.'

'Thank you. Once again, my lord, thank you for your hospitality. Will you convey our best wishes to Mrs Bascombe and tell her we hope for a speedy recovery.'

'I shall do so. Good day, Major Pirie, Mrs Bascombe.'

He bowed and stepped back.

'What a pleasant couple,' said Lord Ryde, watching the carriage rattle away.

'Indeed, my lord.'

'Please can you send Miss Fairburn to Mrs Bascombe and then ask Sir William and Mr Martin to join me in the library.'

'At once, my lord.'

'And you too, Porlock, if you please.'

Chapter Eleven

Mrs Bascombe was barely aware of being helped to her room. Pausing on the threshold, she stared blindly, as if she had never seen it before. Tiller, who had not seen that look on her face for many years, closed her mouth on what she had been going to say and at once bustled forward.

'I have no idea what has happened,' whispered Miss Fairburn. 'I believe she received visitors – two strangers – who have since departed.'

'Best leave her to me, miss,' said Tiller, gruffly. 'She shouldn't be up. I told her so. I'll try to get her to lie down a little.'

'Yes, please,' said Lady Elliott. 'I am convinced she has not yet recovered from her wound.'

'Was it bad news? Did they bring bad news, my lady? A member of her family, perhaps'

'I really don't know. I shall go now to speak to his lordship. Miss Fairburn, will you accompany me?'

Laura hesitated, torn between curiosity and loyalty.

Tiller, who wanted Mrs Bascombe to herself, and was agog to know what had occurred downstairs, ushered them both gently but firmly out of the door.

When she turned back, worryingly, Mrs Bascombe was exactly as she had left her.

Alternately coaxing and cajoling, she got her laid down upon her bed, covering her with a soft blanket, all the while keeping up a gentle commentary on the events of the day, the weather, the state of Ryde House, anything she could think of, because the awful, blank expression on Mrs Bascombe's face alarmed her more than she would admit, even to herself.

She had thought those days were done.

She closed the curtains, shutting out the day and built up the fire. Silence and warmth filled the room. When she looked next, Mrs Bascombe had closed her eyes, so Tiller, supposing her mistress wished to be alone, as was always her preference, quietly withdrew.

When she returned, some twenty minutes later, Mrs Bascombe was gone.

Downstairs, Lord Ryde, along with Sir William and Mr Martin, had just finished issuing instructions to an astonished Porlock, when he glanced out of the window to see Mrs Bascombe making her way towards the lake. That she was in some distress was apparent, even from this distance.

'You go after her,' said Sir William, recovering from his surprise. 'Mr Martin and I will make all the arrangements necessary. Go at once.'

His lordship needed no further urging. He left the room and as hatless as Mrs Bascombe herself, was soon striding across the long grass after her.

The day was blustery and there were spots of rain in the wind. In what state of mind must she be in to be out, without hat or coat, on a day like this? And what were Miss Fairburn or Lady Elliott about to let her do so? Anxiety sharpened his temper.

He found her standing at the end of the old, rickety jetty, staring down into the deep, dark water. A brief inspection confirmed it unlikely to take his weight as well and he dared not approach further. He halted some ten paces away and made himself take two or three deep breaths before speaking softly.

'Elinor, I do believe the jetty is unsafe. Please allow me to take you back to the house.'

She made no response.

He tried again, saying in a slightly brisker tone, 'Actually, I know the jetty is unsafe. It always has been. I vividly

140

remember the last part giving way when I was a very small boy and being precipitated into the water. I know you take great pleasure in regarding me as the brooding hero of romantic legend, and I am sorry to shatter your illusions, but at the time, I had not learned to swim. If it had not been for the prompt action of my governess of the time, a Miss Peabody, who bundled up her petticoats and jumped in after me as I floundered with all the buoyancy of a small rock, I would not be standing here today.'

Still no response.

'Before, however, you consider the commissioning of a small monument to the lady's bravery and dedication to her charge, I should point out that Miss Peabody herself had all the buoyancy of a *large* rock. The two of us were very noisily and splashily drowning when fortunately, one of the gardeners, hearing her screams, came to investigate and was able to pull us both out. However, I believe in giving credit where credit is due and but for her piercing shrieks, we would certainly have drowned. The point I am making, Elinor, is that should you fall in, I think it extremely unlikely I would ever be able to reproduce those extraordinary sounds and thus ensure your rescue. So, I'm begging you, please, come back at once.'

She turned her head. 'I note there is no mention of you jumping in to save me.'

'My dear girl, you cannot be serious! These boots came from Maxwell's in London and you would not believe what they cost me.'

'You could take them off.'

'By which time you would have long since vanished beneath the surface.'

She sighed.

'Enough, Elinor. Come to me.'

He held out his hand.

For a long while, she stood motionless, and then, to his enormous relief, slowly made her way back along the

141

creaking jetty.

He took her hand, and well aware there would be curious eyes watching them both from the house, led her under the fresh green canopy of nearby tree. Taking off his own coat, he draped it gently around her shoulders.

'We should go back to the house,' she said quietly.

'In a moment.'

She stood silently, staring at the ground.

Lord Ryde had never been a man for regret. What was done was done and could never be undone, but he knew now, with great certainty, that if he had anything to offer, anything other than a derelict estate and a disgraced name then he would offer it. Now. This moment. Freely, and with great happiness, but it was twenty years too late for that. The knowledge hit him like a blow.

'Did you love him so very much?'

Her head came up. 'Love him? Yes, of course I did. He was my protector. In a world filled with ... we were naturally thrown together a great deal. He was young and impressionable. I think he saw himself as my parfait, gentil knight. Of course I loved him. I loved him a great deal. I suspect, however, that you mean – was I in love with him? – and the answer is no.'

She went on.

'All this is my fault. If I had managed to escape away to my room as soon as he started to ... That was my usual course of action. I would lock myself in with Tilly and he could rage and bluster all he liked, but he couldn't get in and then he usually wandered off and drank himself unconscious and Porlock would tell us when it was safe to come out. I just didn't move fast enough that night. If I had been able to get away, then George wouldn't have intervened and then he wouldn't have been thrown out, and he wouldn't have gone to Ryde House, and maybe your father wouldn't have died, and you wouldn't be poor and George wouldn't have had to flee – to India, of all places – and he wouldn't have died of fever. He was on his way home. He was coming home. He could have explained what happened. Why would he come home unless he was innocent? And now he's dead.'

Her voice rose sharply at the end.

He said gently, 'You will never convince me about George Bascombe, Elinor. We must agree to differ on that subject. I am sorry he is dead, because I can see his death is causing you great distress and I am sorry for it. I will not insult you by saying perhaps it is all for the best because you will never agree, but it is very possible that he might have been arrested the moment he set foot in England. He – and you – have been spared that. If you want to remember your friend, remember him as a boy, living with you at Westfield. Don't remember that night. Don't even think of it. Find a few happy memories and keep those in your heart instead.'

She dragged a sleeve across her face. The spots of rain fell faster now.

'Is that what you do?'

'I beg your pardon?'

'Is that what you do? Remember only the happy times? And keep them in your heart?'

Now did not seem to be the moment to say that his heart was empty. And besides, he wasn't sure that was true any longer.

'I have seen many things. The Acropolis at dawn. Snow on the Alps. And the Pyrenees. Fields of cherry blossom in the spring. More golden sunsets and rosy-fingered dawns than you can possibly imagine. Strange places and strange people.'

'What an empty answer.'

Of course it was. Because he himself was empty. But, like Mrs Bascombe, he had a streak of resilience.

'Dear God, madam. Much more of this and I'll be plunging into the water with you. Do you think they'll say it was a lovers' pact?'

She stared at him for a moment, shocked and then began

143

to laugh.

And then began to cry.

He let her, simply pulling her further under the tree as she sobbed. And then, as suddenly as it began, it was over. She dragged her sleeve across her nose and sniffed hard.

'You're very damp today, Mrs Bascombe,' said his lordship, matter of factly. 'Soggy, even. Allow me to pass you my handkerchief.'

She took it from him, pantomimed wringing it out, blew her nose, and then tucked it into her sleeve.

'I believe,' he said, 'that on occasions similar to this one, it customary to request the user to keep the usually revolting object. Since you are, of course, aware of my straightened circumstances, I have no hesitation in requesting you to return it with all speed.'

Mrs Bascombe obligingly dragged the handkerchief from her sleeve and offered it to him.

His lordship regarded it and sighed. 'My acquaintanceship with you, Mrs Bascombe, has added new layers to the horrors of poverty. Please keep it.'

Mr Martin, meanwhile, had lost no time in acquainting an astonished Miss Fairburn with the substance of the visit. Miss Fairburn's first thought was that if she and Elinor had to leave Westfield then it really made very little difference whether Mr Martin went to America or not, and immediately reproached herself for her selfishness. She had always said she would never leave Elinor and how much more would she cling to her now there was the possibility they must find a new home.

Lady Elliot, hearing that Sir William had to return to Rushford on urgent business took such news in her stride. As the spouse of a serving Justice of the Peace, she was aware that these things frequently happened. She was, in any case, far more interested in the day's events at Ryde House.

She, Mr Martin, and Miss Fairburn were sitting in the

drawing room, discussing the events of the day. Mr Martin was explaining, not for the first time, that the Major and his sister were actually extremely pleasant people who had behaved exactly as they ought and had certainly shown no signs of pushing themselves forwards.

'Their behaviour towards Mrs Bascombe showed the greatest respect and discretion,' he said. 'She may remain at Westfield for as long as she wishes. They made a strong plea for her to make her home with them, should she wish to do so. I believe it was the news of Mr Bascombe's death, rather than their actual appearance which caused Mrs Bascombe such distress.'

Miss Fairburn went again to the window to peer anxiously across the grass in search of her friend. Lady Elliott, however, more than slightly mollified by Mr Martin's words, was engaging in a little wishful thinking. Major Pirie was, after all, a single man, not much above thirty, if that, and the arrival of a single man in such a restricted neighbourhood ... She began to calculate how long before Clara was out and whether it would be advantageous to bring Louisa, undoubtedly the prettier of the two, out at the same time. She was roused from this reverie by the sound of footsteps on the gravel outside.

'They're back,' said Mr Martin.

They were admitted by the ever-watchful Porlock, who subjected his mistress to a discreet inspection, drew her to one side, and said, 'I wonder if I might have a word with you, madam?'

Yes, of course, Porlock. What is it?'

'Are you feeling better, ma'am?'

'Yes, thank you. Much better,' said Elinor, feeling anything but.

'Well, the thing is, ma'am ... with everything as uncertain as it is at the moment ... everything is changing – which is natural and right, but I wanted to say ...' he paused again, and then with some difficulty continued, 'I think today has brought home to us all that the old days, for whatever reason, are drawing to an end. Mrs Stokesley and I – well, ma'am, we had always hoped one day to be serving Mr George – and possibly Mr George's children, too. Well, I think it inevitable that whatever transpires from today's events, nothing will be the same afterwards. One day there will be new people at Westfield. Young people, probably, and not to put too fine a point on it, Mrs Stokesley and I – we're not as young as we were and so I wanted to say, when you leave Westfield, ma'am, that Mrs Stokesley and I would count it a privilege to be allowed to accompany you. It is a pleasure to serve you, ma'am, wherever you go. And we thought that having us with you would be beneficial to us all. We could – ease each other through difficult times, as it were.'

She stared at the floor for some moments until she was able to command her voice and then laid her hand on his forearm and said, 'Let us hope it does not come to that, my dear friend, but if it does ...' she stopped again. The magnitude of such an offer was not lost on her. Both Porlock and Stokesley had served at Westfield nearly all their lives. Mrs Stokesley had been born on the estate. Westfield had been their home for so long ... what could she possibly say to such an offer? It was impossible to tell them she could not afford to take them with her. That the sum of six pounds, thirteen shillings and fourpence was all she had or was ever likely to have in the entire world. That it was possible that Porlock had more money in a sock under his bed than she herself possessed. But an offer had been made – a staggeringly generous offer and she must respond.

'Thank you, Porlock. And please thank Mrs Stokesley, too. I am honoured that you should feel ...'

She pulled herself together.

'Whatever happens, I shall never forget what you have said. Thank you, my dear friend.'

He nodded, much moved himself, and melted away to the servants' quarters.

Lord Ryde, who had paused in the shadows to take a pinch of snuff, returned his box to his pocket and watched in silence as she crossed the hall and entered the library.

He was tempted – strongly tempted – to request the favour of an interview with Mrs Bascombe at that very moment. There were things that should be said to her but it would not do. There had been enough high-flown emotion today. There would be time enough later on. He himself needed a period of quiet and he was certain Mrs Bascombe did as well.

Entering the library in her wake, he found Mr Martin, Miss Fairburn, and Lady Elliott setting themselves up for a not very serious game of vingt-et-un.

Drawing her near to the fire, he said, 'What do you say, Mrs Bascombe? Shall we leave them to their trivial pursuits? Do you play chess, ma'am?'

'I do, sir. I play reasonably well.'

'I daresay, ma'am, but do you play well enough to challenge me?'

'How often our thoughts run together, my lord,' she replied amiably. 'I was just thinking the same thing about you.'

As he had hoped, this bracing treatment brought a little colour to her cheeks. They settled themselves before the fire and he laid out the pieces.

'Black or white?'

'Black,' she said, with something of a snap.

She took the first game easily, suspecting all the time that he was letting her win, and cast a mocking glance at him as they reassembled the board.

'It would seem our questions have been answered.'

'Not necessarily,' he replied. 'Your move, ma'am.'

He won the second game – just. He suspected this was mostly because Mrs Bascombe method of play was very

147

similar to her style of riding. Her strategy consisted of hurling all her pieces forwards simultaneously and annihilating everything in her path. Backed into a corner, his king fought for his life, surviving only because eventually Mrs Bascombe ran out of pieces and was forced to concede.

'One each, ma'am,' he remarked. 'Shall we play the deciding game?'

'Of course.'

He crossed to the table to pour them both a glass of wine and glanced around the room as she again set up the board.

Outside, the rain hammered against the windows. The curtains, drawn already against, shut out the weather and made the room cosy. At the other end, the three gamesters, alternately winning and losing colossal sums of make-believe money to each other, laughed and argued with the ease of people who enjoyed each other's company. The room suited candlelight. The colours of the once good Turkish carpet glowed gently in their light. Furniture gleamed. The room smelled of old leather, wood smoke, and polish. It was, his lordship reflected, a very pleasant way to spend an inclement afternoon. He had a sudden vision of many such afternoons, sitting before a comfortable fire, playing chess with a small lady, whose fair hair gleamed in the firelight; who was soft and warm and loving and stung like a bee.

A shout of mixed laughter and dismay from the cardsharps recalled him to his surroundings. He blinked to find Mrs Bascombe watching him. For a moment, his breath stopped.

He smiled at her. She smiled back.

'Prepare to meet your doom, my lord.'

He sighed. The warning was far too late. Far, far too late.

Chapter Twelve

As Lord Ryde had hoped, worn out by their day, the ladies retired immediately after dinner, leaving the gentlemen to their port. Porlock, pausing by the door to ensure everything was in order, caught his lordship's eye, nodded once, and softly withdrew.

Feeling the need for some solitary contemplation, Elinor dismissed Tiller as soon as she could, closing the door on her protests. Calling goodnight to Miss Fairburn, she wearily prepared for bed and blew out her candle.

Throughout the house, the lights were extinguished, one by one.

Silence fell.

The house slept.

Elinor, asleep almost as soon as her head touched her pillow, was jolted awake by an unmistakeable pistol shot. And another. Then two more in quick succession. For a second, she was almost paralysed with fear, and then swung her legs out of bed, groping for her dressing gown. Seizing her oil lamp, she turned up the wick with trembling fingers and wrenched open her bedroom door, almost colliding with Miss Fairburn who stood on the threshold.

Sounds of an altercation could clearly be heard. What seemed an enormous number of male voices shouting, together with the crash of overturning furniture gave the impression of a major engagement being fought.

'Quickly!' hissed Miss Fairburn.

'Wait,' whispered Elinor and re-entering her room, armed herself with a useful looking poker.

'Excellent idea,' said Miss Fairburn, helping herself to a particularly vicious-looking coal shovel.

They were met on the landing by Lady Elliott – a vision in a voluminous wrapper and a very pretty lace cap, slightly askew. Elinor braced herself for a scolding, but the light of battle was in Lady Elliott's eye. Catching sight of her two armed companions, she went at once to Elinor's fireplace. Finding, to her disappointment, that the most obvious implements had already been selected, she had, perforce to make do with the coal-tongs, although no one catching sight of the dangerous jut of her chin could doubt her intent to wield them in the most dangerous way imaginable.

'Enough is enough,' she hissed. 'Ladies – forward!'

The three ladies inched their way down the stairs and across the dim hall. The only light shone from the drawing room, whose open door allowed them to see their way and from which came the sounds of an almighty struggle. His lordship's voice could be heard, raised in wrathful intent. Mr Martin also was clearly audible, shouting instructions to some unknown party. Astonishingly, Elinor thought she could also hear Porlock's majestic tones, all in addition to the sound of crashing furniture and breaking ornaments.

'On three,' instructed Lady Elliott, in much the same tones as Boadicea might have instructed her warriors to wipe St Albans from the face of the earth. Elinor and Laura nodded grimly and took a firm grip on their weapons of choice.

'Three.'

Implements raised, the three ladies burst into the drawing room. An amazing sight met their eyes and it took some seconds for the chaotic scrum to resolve itself into its various component parts.

A single unshaded lantern threw a dim glow across a disordered room. Distorted shadows leaped around the walls. It was obvious that a titanic struggle was taking place.

Lord Ryde and a short, thickset man in a dark coat buttoned to his throat grappled for possession of a wicked-looking pistol, whose silver fittings gleamed in the light. In her initial horror, Elinor at first thought he had no face, until she realised the intruder was wearing a mask. That their struggle was carried out in grim silence only added to the drama.

Another man lay semi-conscious nearby. A shattered pie-crust table bore witness to his particular encounter, from which it seemed the table had emerged with more success.

Her butler, Porlock, his attire somewhat more dishevelled than was usual, his face contorted with rage, knelt astride another, smaller man. Under Mrs Bascombe's astonished gaze, he had a firm grip on his assailant's ears and was repeatedly banging his head on the floor.

Across the other side of the room, Mr Martin struggled valiantly with a larger man wielding a brutal-looking cudgel.

Of Munch, there was no sign.

A fifth man struggled to escape through a shattered window. Correctly apprehending that their priority lay in preventing this escape, the three ladies flew across the room.

Mrs Bascombe and Miss Fairburn seized his coat and dragged the potential escapee back into the melee, where he was set upon by Lady Elliott, wielding the fire tongs with no mercy, unleashing a series of poorly-directed but enthusiastic blows upon his person. His screams only added to the confusion.

Having assured herself that this particular intruder was unlikely to cause any further trouble, Mrs Bascombe turned her attention to Lord Ryde's assailant. Too keyed up to feel fear, she hovered, poker raised, awaiting her opportunity. When Lord Ryde was sent reeling by a wildly swinging lucky punch, she saw her opportunity, fetching his opponent a telling blow across his kidneys and following up her advantage with three or four well-directed wallops across his shoulders.

Miss Fairburn, meanwhile was alternately whacking and poking indiscriminately with her weapon of choice, until Mr Martin, who had sustained a few of the more undirected blows himself, laid out his opponent with a neat left and right. He stood panting and nearly spent, but did, however, retain the presence of mind to remove the shovel from his love before she inflicted any permanent damage.

Lord Ryde's adversary had dropped to the floor, curling into a ball in self-defence while Mrs Bascombe, with a cheerful disregard for her injured shoulder, laid about her with the poker. His screams and pleas for mercy were terrible to hear, and possibly feeling some sympathy for his fellow man, Lord Ryde gently detached the poker from her grasp.

Sir William Elliot, entering the room to render assistance and with two stout fellows at his back was astonished to find his wife, attired only in her nightwear and with her cap even more askew than before, belabouring a sinister individual dressed in rough clothes and a face mask.

'Lady Elliott! Madam!'

Lady Elliott paid him no heed. 'And take that, you miscreant. And that, you scoundrel. Villain! Reprobate! Criminal! My husband is a Justice of the Peace and he will have you imprisoned. Or transported. Or hanged.'

Sir William perceived the time had come to save a life.

'Leonora. My dear. He is quite unconscious. You may desist.'

Trembling with rage, Lady Elliott, drew herself to her full height. Her cap now hung down her back and her hair was in wild disarray.

'Sir William. I am so pleased to see you. I insist you arrest these criminals at once. Enough is enough, I say. I declare we are not safe in our beds.'

She broke off. Her voice trembled. Her husband wrested the blood-stained fire- tongs from her grasp.

'You are quite safe now, my dear. I give you my word. I shall have them removed forthwith. The wagon is outside. Fletcher – load them up. You may safely leave it all to me, Leonora. My lord, I trust everyone is uninjured.'

Lord Ryde, who had been subjecting his comrades in arms to a discreet inspection, mopped a trail of blood from his nose and assured Sir William that he and his guests were comparatively unharmed.

'Were you able to apprehend the Piries?'

Sir William nodded. 'Oh yes. I knew they wouldn't be far away. We caught up with them just outside of Whittington. They had no idea we were on to them and were taken completely by surprise.'

As were the rest of the company. He was regarded with astonishment and awe.

Mrs Bascombe found her voice first. 'The Piries? What have they to do with housebreaking?'

Sir William interposed. 'By your leave, Lord Ryde. I must oversee the removal of these people to Rushford.' With a glint of humour, he added, 'I'll leave you to your guests who, no doubt, will be agog to hear details of the events in which they have become embroiled.'

It could only be Lord Ryde's inner demon which prompted him to say, 'Indeed, sir, but I think the wisest course of action would be for the ladies to retire for the night. Mr Martin and I must lock up after you. Porlock, secure the shutters over that window, if you would be so good. I think we should all meet at breakfast and then we can regale the ladies with such information as we deem suitable for them to hear.'

Mrs Bascombe, recognising the glint in Lord Ryde's eye, said nothing, but for one precarious moment, it was entirely possible that Lady Elliott might resume her activities with the fire tongs.

She was deflected (probably deliberately) by her husband, who took her hand, kissed it, and recommended she take herself off to her bedchamber and not worry about anything until the morning.

Lady Elliott, an admirable wife of nearly twenty-five years standing, agreed this was an excellent idea, waited until her husband had left the room and then planted herself on a dilapidated sofa, declaring she would not move until she knew the whole. Mrs Bascombe and Miss Fairburn ranged themselves on either side of her and contrived, entirely without words, to suggest that nothing short of brute force would shift them.

Porlock discreetly adjusted his clothing to his satisfaction and informed his lordship that no doubt the entire household had been roused by the commotion and that he would take it upon himself to reassure the staff and send in a tea tray.

'Thank you, Porlock,' said Mrs Bascombe, warmly.

Crunching his way across broken china and splintered furniture, he moved majestically to the door.

Lord Ryde was recalled to his duties as a host. 'Ladies, I suggest we repair to the library, where, I believe, there is a fire, and we shall certainly be more comfortable.'

Candles had been lit in the library, and Margaret, as sensible in her choice of nightwear as she was with daywear, was viciously puffing away with the bellows in a manner that led Lord Ryde to reflect that, unbelievably, he did still have something to be thankful for.

'Now,' said Lady Elliot, seating herself on the sofa with a determined air, 'the full story, please, Lord Ryde, and never mind sparing our sensibilities. After this evening, I doubt I have any left.'

Lord Ryde took up a position in front of the fireplace and wondered where on earth to begin.

'Would I be right in assuming, said Mrs Bascombe, carefully, 'that the appearance of the Piries and the events of this evening are not unconnected?'

'It seems safe to do so. I myself am of the opinion that a large and very professional team of housebreakers have, for reasons which are completely beyond me at the moment, targeted this establishment.'

His guests remembered their manners and did not stare about them in astonishment at such folly.

'But how,' demanded Lady Elliot, mother of five children and accustomed to getting to the bottom of things, 'how did you know that?'

'Really ma'am, I am unsure how to proceed without making my part in these sorry proceedings more important than it actually is.'

'Try,' said Mrs Bascombe, tartly.

'Well, the disguise of Major Pirie and his sister was, I have to say, perfect. Their manners, demeanour, sentiments, all were exactly as we could have wished and it was not until their departure that I had any idea they were not exactly who they said they were.'

'How?' demanded Elinor. 'I saw nothing amiss. What gave them away?'

'Do not tease yourself, Mrs Bascombe. You were not actually present when the Major made his one small slip.'

'Which was?'

'During a conversation, Major Pirie let slip they had not called in at Westfield.'

He paused to take a pinch of snuff.

The room was silent.

'Well?' demanded Lady Elliot.

'They were not driving a local carriage. In fact, they had come directly from Hereford.'

Still, his listeners regarded him in bafflement.

His lordship gave them another clue. 'They did not call in at the Red Lion.'

'Good heavens,' said Mrs Bascombe. 'Of course!'

'Of course what?' said Miss Fairburn. 'Why is that so important? I warn you all now – I shall have strong hysterics if everything is not explained immediately.'

His lordship drew breath to speak, but Mrs Bascombe got there first.

'If they did not break their journey in the village,' she said slowly, 'how did they know I was here at Ryde House? Why did they not call at Westfield first? It's what anyone

155

would have done. They didn't and therefore …'

She seemed unable to continue.

'And therefore,' said Lord Ryde gently, 'they must have known of your injury before they arrived in the neighbourhood and the only way they could know that was if they themselves were involved.'

She paled a little. 'So I was the target after all? But why?'

'I'm afraid we are no nearer to ascertaining the truth of the matter at the moment, but I am sure Sir William's people will have some expertise in extracting information from reluctant sources. I suggest we drink our tea and then the ladies return to their chambers and try to sleep. You, especially, Mrs Bascombe, have had a very trying day.'

'Wait,' said Mrs Bascombe, who had been sitting, lost in thought. 'Does this mean – what about George? Is he married or not?'

His lordship gently removed her cup and saucer and set it upon a side table. 'I'm very much afraid, Mrs Bascombe, that Miss Pirie, or whatever she calls herself, has never been married to Mr Bascombe. There is certainly no child. I suspect that somewhere or other, they heard the story of what happened at Ryde House and somehow thought they could capitalise on the events of all those years ago. If it is of any consolation in this confusing time, you have no reason to quit Westfield, which can continue to remain your home.'

Mrs Bascombe was barely aware of his words.

Lady Elliot, who had been watching her carefully, rose to her feet. 'Elinor, my love, I think it is time to retire. The gentlemen will need to secure the house and for that, they will not need our help. Come.'

Miss Fairchild and Mrs Bascombe rose obediently. Lord Ryde saw them to the door.

'Please try and sleep, Mrs Bascombe. There will be time and more tomorrow for all this to be properly examined. You will do yourself no good lying awake for what remains of the night. At present, we do not even know the questions, let alone the answers.'

She smiled and slipped into the hall.

'Miss Fairchild, good night and thank you.'

As Lady Elliot drew near, however, he took her hand and kissed it. 'Ma'am, I knew the moment I clapped eyes on you, that you were a force to be reckoned with and tonight's events have proved me to be correct. May I express the heartfelt plea that, in future, you and I are always on the same side. I am convinced that you pounding that unfortunate fellow into submission with nothing but a set of fire-tongs will live in his nightmares – and possibly those of his associates – for the rest of his life. Lady Elliot, Mrs Bascombe, Miss Fairburn – you were magnificent!'

Blushing, the three ladies retired to their bedchambers.

Breakfast was served the next morning at noon. Mrs Bascombe, Miss Fairburn, and Lady Elliot all arrived together. Lord Ryde and Mr Martin rose at their entrance and wished them good morning.

'Barely,' remarked Lady Elliott with a glance at the clock on the mantel. 'Really, one feels quite ashamed at the lateness of the hour.'

'Quite,' murmured Lord Ryde, himself no stranger to reluctant midday rising.

The day was fine and sunny. Sunshine streamed through the windows as a slightly battered Porlock supervised servings of warm rolls, preserves, a plate of fine ham, and a dish of fruit. Margaret and Janet flew from sideboard to table and back again, and for a while, conversation was at a minimum as each person seated themselves and somewhat to their own surprise made a substantial breakfast.

Lord Ryde, keeping an unobtrusive eye on a strangely quiet Mrs Bascombe, enquired whether he might pour her another cup of coffee. She nodded her thanks, but it was obvious her thoughts were many miles away. His lordship had no difficulty identifying the busy thoughts running through her head and waited for her to speak. Around the table, as if by an unseen signal, the conversations slowly died away and faces turned towards the head of the table.

Mrs Bascombe turned to Lord Ryde. 'George is not dead, is he?'

Even after everything that had happened, he noted, her first thoughts were still for George Bascombe.

'If you disregard the false statements made by the Piries – and I think we can – then no, George Bascombe is not dead.'

She bent her head over her plate. 'But, we have no evidence that he is alive, do we?'

He said carefully, 'No, we have no knowledge of whether Mr Bascombe is alive or dead and, therefore, I beg you not to agitate yourself for no reason, Mrs Bascombe.'

'No,' she said, briskly, sitting up and squaring her shoulders. 'In fact we are in exactly the same position as we were last week. Nothing has changed in any way.'

Lord Ryde, for whom everything had changed in the last seven days, refrained from comment.

'So tell me about the events of last night,' said Miss Fairburn to Mr Martin. 'I presume you laid a trap for those men.'

'We did indeed. On Lord Ryde's instructions, Porlock locked up the house as usual, turned out the lights and we all retired to the library with the door ajar to await events. Roberts and Owen were concealed in the vast amounts of overgrown shrubbery with which, happily, Ryde House is so abundantly provided and Sir William and his men waited with the wagon.'

He paused for a dramatic sip of coffee. Lord Ryde took a moment to admire his secretary's storytelling abilities. The ladies all regarded him with bated breath.

'And?' demanded Mis Fairburn. 'What happened? At what time did they appear? What did you do?'

'I have to say, ma'am, that they were an extremely

professional crew. We heard barely the faintest snick as they forced a latch. If we had not all been listening for such a sound, we might well have missed it. As it was, we crept forward across the darkened hall and surprised them in the very act.'

He paused again and Porlock stepped forwards to refill his cup.

'Yes,' said Lady Elliot, breathlessly. 'And what happened next?'

'Well, ma'am, I cannot speak for my companions, but I was greatly taken aback by the number of intruders in the room and only the fact that Porlock was between me and the door prevented me from running from the room in terror.'

Lady Elliott made a noise that could only have been copied from one of her younger sons. The company tactfully ignored it.

'No, truthfully, ma'am. We were astonished that there were so many of them. Surely such a large gang cannot be normal?'

He turned to Lord Ryde as he spoke, who put down his cup.

'Why are you all looking at me? I am flattered at your apparent belief in my boundless knowledge of housebreaking, but I do assure you, my familiarity with this subject is very slight. Nevertheless, Charles is correct and had I had the faintest inkling of their numbers, I would never have undertaken such a venture and placed us all at such risk. I really must apologise and –'

He paused. In the distance, the bell rattled another death-throe. Porlock moved regally towards the door, but before he could reach it, Munch ushered in another guest.

'Sir William Elliott, my lord.'

Lord Ryde rose. 'Sir William, you are most welcome. I hope you have some information for us. Porlock, a chair and some breakfast for our guest, please.'

Sir William, always punctilious, greeted his wife and

enquired how she had slept. He seated himself beside her and addressed himself to the remains of the ham. Since he had obviously been up all night, the company was obliged to restrain their impatience while he ate his breakfast and drank two cups of coffee.

Finally, he sat back and patted his mouth with his napkin.

'Thank you, Ryde. I don't know when a breakfast has been more welcome. Yes, another cup, please, Porlock.'

'I do hope, Sir William, that you have some information for us. The ladies are agog, and we gentlemen barely less so. I gather that Major Pirie and his sister are all part of this strange affair?'

Sir William allowed his coffee cup to be refilled again. 'As a matter of fact, not brother and sister at all. Not even related. He's Lionel Thorpe, an ex-military man, though not commissioned, and the lady rejoices in the name of Marjorie Bentwater. There's no doubt they've recently journeyed from India, probably just one jump ahead of the authorities all the way, and I think we can conclude that they have met Mr Bascombe at some point in their travels. How long ago that might have been, we have been unable to determine.'

Lord Ryde laid down his napkin. 'But how did they hope to get away with this imposture, Sir William? Surely legal documents would have to be produced?'

'Indeed they would and the reports I have of the efficiency Mrs Bascombe's man of business lead me to assume they would be very carefully scrutinised. The deception could not possibly have been maintained for very long.'

'So what was the point?' said Mr Martin, bewildered. 'If they had burgled Westfield, for instance, especially since half its inhabitants are here – well that makes sense. But Ryde House is positively bulging with occupants at this particular moment.'

Heroically, Lord Ryde refrained from nodding in mournful agreement. In the distance, the bell rattled again and Porlock, determined not to be outmanoeuvred this time, trod from the room with rather more speed than usual.

'Does this mean,' demanded Mrs Bascombe, emerging from the deep thoughts in which she had been indulging, 'that they did not mean to shoot *me* after all?'

'I fear,' said his lordship, gravely, 'that your previous assumption is correct. It would seem that I was the target and you, Mrs Bascombe, were simply – in the way.'

He raised his hand at the babble of protest from around the table.

'Yes, yes, Mrs Bascombe, I quite understand your indignation. It is indeed very galling to be shot in mistake for someone else, but I am sure, when you have had time to consider this sensibly and rationally, you will be able to view these recent events with your usual sense of proportion.'

Mrs Bascombe's was not the only bosom swelling in wrath at this remark, but his lordship swept on.

'The time has come, I think, to put these unfortunate events behind us. An attempt was made to burgle my home – an unsuccessful attempt, fortunately – and in order to facilitate this endeavour, an attempt was made on my life, which went wrong, and Mrs Bascombe was shot instead. Yes, I agree, Mrs Bascombe. Very reprehensible, but those responsible have been apprehended and we can all of us take comfort in the knowledge that the worst is over.'

He was obliged to raise his voice for the latter part of this speech. Sounds of a disturbance could be heard in the hall. Several voices were raised. The company could make out the wheezy tones of Munch in counterpoint to the plummy tones of Porlock. There was the sound of a scuffle and of a table scraping across the floor.

'Good God,' cried Mr Martin. 'Are they fighting?'

He rose to his feet, but before he could move away from the table, the door flew open and the company was treated to the incredible sight of two elderly men locked in apparently mortal combat.

161

'I'll have you know, Mr Porlock, that this is my house and as such it is my place to announce his lordship's visitors.'

And I'll have you know, Mr Munch, that since this visitor is for Mrs Bascombe, it is my place to …'

At this point, both became simultaneously aware of the company regarding them in astonishment.

It was Munch who found his voice first. Unfortunately, he squandered his opportunity by voicing his complaints concerning the encroaching ways of one whom he would not demean himself by naming, but was not standing too far away at that very moment and –

Porlock, however, was made of sterner stuff and would in no way be deflected from the course of his duty. Straightening his clothing, he drew himself to his full height and although in the greatest state of perturbation anyone could ever remember seeing him, announced proudly, and in ringing tones:

'Mr George Bascombe, ma'am.'

Chapter Thirteen

During the course of his travels, his lordship had seen many strange sights and heard many strange stories. One of these had concerned a woman of such supreme ugliness and evil that her very glance was enough to turn all those who encountered it to stone.

It was very possible, reflected his lordship, looking around the room, that this lady had strolled through his dining room only seconds previously, so frozen in astonishment were its occupants.

As for the recently announced Mr Bascombe, it was unlikely that he had expected cries of unbridled delight and surprise at his unexpected appearance. He may even have braced himself for horror and disbelief. What he obviously did not expect, however, was the stunned silence that greeted his entrance. Indeed, he could have been forgiven for believing he had mistakenly entered a room full of statues.

Following hard on the heels of the two ancient, battle-locked retainers, he drew up short under the combined gaze of, including the servants, some ten people, all frozen in astonishment at this unexpected turn of events.

Lord Ryde's first thought was that there must have been some mistake. There could not possibly have been a greater contrast between his memory of big, thickset, untidy Ned Bascombe, with his dark eyes and brows; and the slim, precisely dressed man standing uncertainly before them all.

He saw a slight figure, a little below average height, whose blond curls, bleached even lighter by the sun, were already receding from a high forehead. A deep suntan enhanced his blue eyes, which were, at present, urgently

163

scanning the room. His lordship could guess why and deliberately took a slow, calming breath and released his grip on the arm of his chair.

It did his temper no good at all to see that Mr Bascombe's clothes, although travel-stained, bore every sign of quality and taste. He had, however, the look of a man who had come a long way in as short a time as humanly possible. He looked tired and to his lordship's experienced eye, slightly feverish.

For a long time, no one moved or spoke. The sound of a door opening and closing in some other part of the building and of Mrs Munch barking instructions to some hapless underling could be heard very clearly in the silence.

It was Mrs Bascombe who broke the spell.

'George!'

Leaping to her feet and entirely ignoring her toppled chair, she ran to him with outstretched arms.

'Elinor!' He seized her hands.

'Oh, Georgie – you're not dead.'

'No, dash it, Elinor, of course I'm not,' he said somewhat unsteadily. 'Not dead yet, although I've come close once or twice. And quite recently as well. But you? How do you do? You look so well, but they told me you were hurt. That you'd been shot. By God, Elinor, I got her as quickly as I could, but I'm too late and feared the worst when they told me at Westfield.'

'I am well, George. Almost completely recovered. And much, much better now that you are here. But why are you here? I was never so pleased to see anyone in my life, but how do you come to arrive at such an opportune moment?'

'Yes, Mr Bascombe,' said Lord Ryde, breaking his long silence. He had not risen to greet his new guest. 'Pray tell how you come to arrive at this more than opportune moment?'

His tone of voice was not lost on Mr Bascombe, who put Elinor gently to one side and advanced up the room.

'Lord Ryde, I assume?'

164

'I congratulate you on your entirely accurate assumption and wait with some interest to hear on what grounds you could possibly consider yourself welcome in my house?'

Elinor stood rooted to the dingy carpet with shock. Carried away in the joy of George's return, she had quite naturally assumed that everyone else would be as pleased to see him as she was herself. This was not, however, the case. Glancing now at Lord Ryde, she noted the deepening lines around his mouth and heard the hard note in his voice. So had he looked on pulling himself out of his ditch, on the first day they met. Until this moment, she had not realised how far he had come.

She was not the only one. Mr Martin was also familiar with the fortunately infrequent signs of his lordship's anger. He flicked his gaze to Sir William, who nodded his understanding.

Mr Bascombe pulled himself together with an effort. 'I must apologise for bursting into your house so unexpectedly.'

'Not at all, Mr Bascombe. After all, bursting into Ryde House unexpectedly is something of a habit with you, is it not?'

With true heroism, Porlock threw himself into the breach. 'Perhaps, Mr Bascombe, sir, you would care to take a seat?'

He was already righting Mrs Bascombe's chair. Miss Fairburn thankfully moved further down the table to the safety of Mr Marin's orbit. He smiled reassuringly at her, but a line deepened between his eyes.

For a moment, it all hung in the balance. Lord Ryde sprawled in his chair, casually playing with his fork. Mr Bascombe stood nearby, a patch of angry red on each cheek.

'If you please, Mr Bascombe,' murmured Porlock and holding his lordship's gaze, Mr Bascombe allowed himself to be seated next to Elinor, who grasped his hand.

A sigh ran around the room as several people who had had not realised they were holding their breath, let it go in

165

relief.

The awkward silence was broken by Porlock requesting to know whether Mr Bascombe would prefer tea or coffee.

'Tea, Porlock, if you would be so good.'

Porlock ushered the extremely reluctant Margaret and Janet from the room and moved smoothly to comply.

Elinor, not insensitive to the cross-currents running around the room, turned eagerly towards Mr Bascombe.

'Georgie, please, you must tell me at once. Why are you here? Where have you been? Please, I feel as if my head will burst.' And indeed, she had suddenly grown alarmingly pale. Lord Ryde signalled to Porlock.

'Would you like a little brandy, Mrs Bascombe? Just a sip, ma'am?'

Elinor could not help laughing.

'Brandy, Lord Ryde? At breakfast?'

'It is gone noon, Mrs Bascombe.'

'The fact that breakfast is taking place at gone noon does not make it any more acceptable, sir.'

'On the contrary, ma'am, I have frequently breakfasted on nothing else and the figure you see sitting before you is, I think, more than adequate testimony as to its efficacy.'

She could not help laughing and some colour returned to her cheeks.

Sir William, who had been watching all of this with close attention, turned an astonished gaze on his wife who blandly returned his stare with an expression of complete innocence.

Resolving to exchange more than a few words with his life's partner at her earliest convenience, he echoed Mrs Bascombe's request for information. 'For you must see, sir, that your appearance here today has caused the liveliest ... curiosity. That you should arrive today of all days – after the events of last night ...'

Lord Ryde spoke again. 'Sir William speaks for himself. I find myself regarding your appearance today with the liveliest suspicion, rather than curiosity. But then, that is what you do, is it not, Mr Bascombe? You make the dramatic appearance and then disappear mysteriously but not, of course, unprofitably, into the night?'

A gasp ran around the table. Flushed with rage, Mr Bascombe tried to get to his feet but was restrained by Mrs Bascombe, herself conscious of anger and some other emotion. Deep disappointment, perhaps.

'George, no, wait. Please. Lord Ryde was the victim of a housebreaking last night and ...'

'But that's why I'm here,' said Mr Bascombe, interrupting her without ceremony, 'Although I regret that I appear to have arrived too late.'

'Too late for what? To participate? To facilitate?'

'By God, sir ...'

'Stop!'

The single word rang around the room like a pistol shot. Sir William was on his feet.

'Mr Bascombe, please be seated. Lord Ryde, I hesitate to command you in your own home, but I would remind all of you that with the authority vested in me as Justice of the Peace, I am investigating the crime that has taken place here and I will get to the bottom of the events of last night. And possibly the events of some years ago as well.'

Silence fell.

'Thank you. Mr Bascombe, please be good enough to start at the beginning. Why are you here today? For what purpose have you returned?'

Mr Bascombe appeared to make a huge effort to speak quietly. 'I understand you have suffered from housebreakers?'

'I have,' said Lord Ryde, evenly. 'We were seriously incommoded by a large gang last night, who appear to have been led by a respectable couple calling themselves Major Pirie and Mrs George Bascombe. Sir William has been trying to extract more information from them but with small success.'

'Well, no need for that. I can tell him everything he needs to know about that precious pair.'

'Indeed? Why am I unsurprised to find you on apparently intimate terms with this pair of fraudulent housebreakers?'

Obviously keeping his temper with an effort, Mr Bascombe replied, 'Because I met them on the *Athena* when I was returning from India.'

'India,' cried Mrs Bascombe. 'So you have been living in India, after all?'

'Well of course I have, Nell. Look at the colour of me.'

'But how did you come to be in India?'

'Mrs Bascombe,' said Sir William, heavily.

'I beg your pardon, sir. Continue, George.'

'Perhaps,' said Sir William, glancing at the faces around the table, 'it might be best if you begin at the very beginning. I'm sorry, Mrs Bascombe, if this will cause you any distress. Perhaps,' he added hopefully, 'you would prefer to wait in your room?'

A small sound emanated from Lord Ryde and was not missed by Mrs Bascombe.

'No, Sir William. I thank you for your consideration, but I would not prefer to wait in my room. Go on, Georgie. Right from the beginning.'

'Are you sure, Elinor?' he said, softly.

'I am.'

'In that case, I wonder if I might take up Lord Ryde's very kind offer of a breakfast brandy.'

Lord Ryde flicked his eyes to Porlock and nodded.

'Well,' said Mr Bascombe. 'Where to begin?'

Since it was apparent the question was rhetorical, the company remained silent.

He sipped his brandy and set the glass in front of him with some deliberation. Taking a deep breath and not looking at anyone, he spoke to his glass.

'Ned had been in a foul mood all day so I took myself off. I shouldn't have done so, but my presence seemed to irritate

168

him all the more, so I took a gun and went after rabbits. I seem to remember I bagged a few. Well, I must have, because I dropped my bag and dirty coat off in the gun room and walked down the corridor to the rest of the house. I could hear Ned long before I saw him.'

Without looking, he groped for Elinor's hand. The two of them sat silently, reliving bad memories.

'He was … not behaving well towards Elinor … and I went to intervene. There was an argument. He was very drunk. I … in fact he was like a man possessed. I did what I could, but he was a big man and he just picked me up by the scruff of the neck … like some mongrel pup … and threw me out of the door. I rolled over and tried to get back into the house and the next thing I knew, he was pointing a pistol at me. Heaven knows where it had come from. He was only about ten feet away. He couldn't miss. I saw Elinor seize his arm and struggle with him. She shouted at me to run away. I didn't want to.' He turned to Elinor and took her hands. At that moment, there were only the two of them in the room.

'I know, Georgie,' she said softly. 'I understand.'

'I left you.'

'You had no choice. He would have killed you. Go on. Tell everyone what happened at Ryde House.'

He sipped at his brandy again.

I set off into the night, heading for Ryde House. I did consider Greystones, Sir William, but it was too far away and …'

'And old Lord Ryde was probably in a much better position to assist,' said Sir William gruffly. 'Good thinking, my boy.'

Elinor glanced at Lord Ryde, who was pouring himself a brandy.

'Anyway,' said Mr Bascombe, 'it was a beastly night and it took me a while to fight my way through the woods. I don't know what Sugden thought when he saw me. I'm surprised he let me in, given the state of me, but let me in he

169

did. He showed me into the library. The old lord was sitting at his desk as he always was.'

He turned to Lord Ryde. 'I know you didn't get on. How much of that was my fault, I don't know. You'd gone abroad before I went to live with Ned and Elinor, so we never met. I only know that he received me with great kindness. He sat me by the fire with a brandy and politely continued with what he had been doing until I was able to speak coherently. I was … cold and frightened … It took me a while to pull myself together. I wanted him to go back to Westfield at once, but he pointed out, quite rightly, that it had taken me the better part of two hours to get to Ryde House and that whatever had happened there was likely over with by now. He did say he would ride over first thing in the morning and give Ned to understand that this sort of behaviour was to cease forthwith. He did everything he could to put my mind at ease. I'm sorry, Elinor, but I was just too tired to argue. And quite honestly, on consideration, he couldn't have gone right at that very moment. I thought he looked very tired and I noticed his hand shaking a little as he pulled out another piece of paper and began to write.

'He sent Sugden to get me some things and told me the best thing I could do was to leave the neighbourhood. Naturally, I protested, but he said Ned wasn't safe to be around any longer. He would take steps to ensure your safety, Elinor, but he was sending me to up to London, out of the way.

'I … I was pretty scared. I knew no one there. I had no idea what I would do when I got there. I had no money. He said he would write to some people he knew. That I would be taken care of. That he would give me some money and I was to catch the mail coach when it stopped in the village. He gave me some money from the safe.'

'Wait,' said Lord Ryde. 'We reach the part of your story that interests me very much. How much money did he give you?'

'He gave me twenty guineas.'

'From the safe?'

'Yes.'

'Which was open?'

'Yes. Not wide open. Just slightly ajar.'

'Did you note the contents of the safe?'

'No.'

'Indeed?'

'No. I was too busy watching Lord Ryde. His hands were shaking so badly he could barely lift his cashbox. I thought he was ill. I wanted to call Sugden.'

'But you didn't?'

'He asked me not to.'

'What was he writing?'

'A letter. I watched him seal it.'

Lord Ryde stared out of the window. Becoming aware of the silence in the room, he gestured. 'Go on.'

Mr Bascombe swallowed.

'I donned a coat, a greatcoat, and hat, pocketed the guineas, thanked him profusely, and left.'

'You left? Just like that?'

'Yes.'

'Did anyone see you leave?'

'No. I went out through the French windows.'

'You didn't return at all?'

'No. How could I? I had to run to catch the mail.'

'And you did catch the mail?'

'I did, yes.'

'Did anyone witness this?'

'Well, obviously the driver, who was suspicious because I had no luggage. Although God knows where he is now. Given the amount of brandy he was putting away, he's probably in the ground, but old Jessop was there. The landlord. And the pot boy. No ostler, because they didn't change the horses, but yes, there were witnesses. But surely all this was investigated at the time?'

He paused, but Lord Ryde had resumed his contemplation of the wilderness outside and said nothing.

'It was a hell of a journey, begging your pardon, ladies, because my adventures had only just begun. Barely had I alighted from the coach in London, when I was caught up in events yet again. The passengers were dispersing. The inn was packed, and I was famished, so I thought I'd try somewhere else. I'd travelled all day, night was drawing in again, my head was spinning with fatigue and hunger, and I needed somewhere to stay, so off I set. There was a portly gentleman ahead of me. I vaguely remembered him from the coach. He'd been inside and I'd been outside so our paths hadn't crossed.

'Anyway, I'd barely registered his presence when two men stepped out of a doorway and clubbed him to the ground. I was so surprised, I acted without thinking – again – ' he added with a rueful smile, 'and barged in to help. I shouted and ran towards them, making as much noise as I could, and they ran off. I helped the gentleman to his feet. He wasn't badly hurt and he didn't live far away, so I took him home. He offered me a meal and a bed for the night, which I gladly accepted.

'To cut a long story short, he was a merchant. A wealthy one, too, with trading interests on the continent and in India. We got to talking the next day and liked the look of each other. He offered me money, which I refused, God knows why, and then he offered me a job.

'Well, you know me, Elinor, a complete dunce at school. I always thought I had the Bascombe brains. Or lack of, but I found I could do it. I had a talent for business. I enjoyed it. I started as a clerk and worked my way up. Two years later, I had a good job in the company, prospects, everything a man could wish for.'

'But George, why did you not write? I was so worried for you. And people were saying such dreadful things about you. Why did you not write and put my mind at rest?'

172

'I did, Elinor. I wrote five or six times. I never received any reply and after a while, I thought I might be doing more harm than good and so I just stopped.'

'But I never saw any of your letters. Why did I not … oh, of course. Ned.'

'He must have intercepted them. I did write, Elinor. I was so worried for you. I tried to make enquiries, but I didn't want to make things any worse if perhaps you and he had … you know … a reconciliation.'

'And when enquiries were made in connection with Lord Ryde's death, my husband lied and said he'd never heard anything from you.'

'Yes,' he said bitterly, 'It would suit him very well to have me unable to return to Westfield – or even this country. Living abroad in want and poverty. But then, I was offered the job in India and of course, I seized it with both hands.

'No,' said Lord Ryde, harshly. 'Enquiries were made. Why did you not come forward and explain?'

Mr Bascombe stared at him. 'If you tell me they were, then I must accept that, I suppose, but it is possible the … net … was not thrown wide enough. While I am sure fashionable London was thoroughly searched for my whereabouts, at the time I was living far across town in a district, which, whilst thoroughly respectable, would certainly have been unknown to those fortunate enough to occupy the more modish part of London. An oversight I daresay, and one I'm sure you would have been able to draw authority's attention to – had you actually been in this country at the time.'

Lord Ryde made to get up but was somehow prevented from doing so by Porlock, who leaned across him to refill his cup. This simple task seemed to take a while, and by the time he had finished, Mr Bascombe was continuing.

'And so I made a new start in a new country.'

'You've been in India all this time?'

'I have indeed. It's a wonderful country, Elinor. I can't

173

wait to tell you all about it.'

'Nor I to hear all about it. But what happened next?'

'Well, the company prospered and I was offered a junior partnership. Very junior, but I accepted the offer and for nearly five years, I did very well. For a young man seeking his fortune, India is the place to be. But, once again, fate took a hand. The old gentleman wrote to me from London – his son was growing up and ready to take his place in the company. He offered to buy back the shares and I was happy to sell them. I'd done all right out of him and his company but I was beginning to feel the need to see England again. To come home. So, I booked a passage on the *Athena*, departing for England via Cape Town. And that, of course, was where I met the Piries.'

He stopped, slowly rotating his glass and staring at the content.

Lord Ryde spoke into the silence. 'Do continue, Mr Bascombe. I am – I'm sure we all are – absolutely agog to hear what happened next.'

'I boarded the *Athena* at the end of November and we set sail. The Piries were both aboard. The weather was not particularly bad, but I retired almost immediately with what I thought was sea-sickness and turned out to be some sort of tropical fever. I'd been out there for years and never succumbed before, so I was particularly aggrieved I should fall ill now. The fever took hold and I was, apparently, quite ill. However, my sufferings were mitigated by the attentions of Mrs Bentwater, Major Pirie's widowed sister. She had, apparently, gained some nursing experience attending her brother on the occasion of a similar fever and with the chaperonage of her maid, offered her services to me. And at the time, jolly glad I was of them, too. However, it must have been during this period that I stupidly babbled of my time here in Rushford, both at Westfield and at Ryde House. In fact, the ship's surgeon told me afterwards that I had been astonishingly chatty about my personal circumstances.

174

'Anyway, I awoke from my delirium at Cape Town, to discover that the Piries had left the ship and booked passage on a newer, faster vessel. I thought nothing of it at the time. It was only when we pulled into port after port that I discovered that neither of them had hesitated to pledge my credit to obtain whatever goods and services they required, and used their unfortunately extensive knowledge of my personal circumstances to live the high life. Everywhere I went, the story was the same. I alerted the authorities and booked passage on the fastest ship I could find. My fear was that they would somehow use their knowledge to gain access to Westfield. I confess, I did not consider Ryde House to be in any danger.

'I finally pulled into England, and pursued them as best I could across country. And I would have caught them too. I was so close, but just outside of Rushford, I suffered a small relapse. Nothing serious, but it kept me in my bed for twenty-four hours. I awoke to find everyone talking of events at Ryde House. I enquired after the nearest Justice of the Peace, discovered he was here, and followed on as quickly as I could. And that's it, Elinor. That's my story.'

He sat back in his chair and closed his eyes.

Porlock bent over him.

'May I fetch you anything else, sir?'

'What? Oh, no, thank you, Porlock. I'm perfectly well now and having discharged my duty, I'll be off the premises and back to Westfield. What of you, Elinor? Are you fit to travel?'

'One moment, please,' said Lord Ryde, and the mood of the room changed again. 'We have been treated to a detailed account of events subsequent to your departure from Ryde House, but I'd like to return, if I may, to the events *prior* to that. Tell me again about the safe.'

Mr Bascombe stared at him. 'Why?'

'Because I wish it.'

'No, I mean, why do you wish it?'

175

'Because I wish to learn its contents.'

'Well I can't tell you what the usual contents were – we weren't that close – but that night, I think it was just the cash box which Lord Ryde used for everyday expenses and the servants' quarter-day wages.''

'Really? So the jewels, the estate documents, the considerable sum of money – all that completely escaped your notice?'

Mr Bascombe stared at him in amazement. Of course they did. What jewels? What money?'

'The jewels and money to which you helped yourself prior to your departure from Ryde House. This London merchant story of yours is just that – a tale hastily concocted to account for the sudden acquisition of a great deal of money. You sudden flight to India bears me out.'

'What sudden flight? I was two years with Mr Jonas Croyde of Croyde, Mellish, and Struther of Cheapside before leaving for India. Ask anyone.'

Sir William intervened. 'You can prove this, Mr Bascombe?'

'Of course I can,' he said, indignantly. 'And in the event of any *official* investigation, I shall be happy to furnish the details. To the proper authorities, of course. Not to any chance-met busybody seeking to cover up his own mismanagement with far-fetched tales of theft.'

Lord Ryde pushed back his chair 'By God, Bascombe. If there were not ladies present I would give you the thrashing you deserve.'

Mr Bascombe flushed furious red with rage. 'You might try, I suppose. And in deference to your age, I might let you land a punch or two, out of charity.'

Both Mr Martin and Sir William were on their feet, but before they could move, Elinor was between the protagonists.

'Enough! Have we not endured enough over these last seven days? Please – both of you – enough.'

She sank slowly back into her chair, very white and trembling.

'My dear Elinor,' Lady Elliot bustled forwards, shooting dagger looks at every unfortunate man in the vicinity. 'Please try to sip a little water. That's very good, my dear. And a little more. Well done.'

She looked at Lord Ryde.

'May I suggest, my lord, since the drawing room still resembles a battlefield at this moment, we should repair to the library? Porlock, I think some fresh tea and coffee would be most beneficial.'

Porlock murmured and withdrew.

'Wait!' said Mr Bascombe, suddenly. 'What do you mean – the drawing room resembles a battlefield?'

Lord Ryde was at his most haughty. 'I'm sorry if most of our conversation has gone over your head, Mr Bascombe. Prior to your arrival, we had been discussing last night's housebreaking.'

'Are you saying they broke into your drawing room? But why?'

'A very good question, Mr Bascombe,' said Sir William. 'That is among the many questions to which I have not yet received satisfactory answers.'

Mr Bascombe leaped to his feet. 'Not the library? They didn't enter the library?'

'No,' said Lord Ryde, slowly. 'Why should they?'

'Because that's where the safe is.'

'That old thing was thrown out many years ago. Anything of value in this house has long since been disposed of.'

'But – oh my God, how can this be? Is it possible you don't know?'

The two men stared at each other. Mr Bascombe was visibly agitated. His flushed face held an expression of the greatest astonishment.

'Know what?' said Lord Ryde hoarsely. 'What don't I know?'

177

'Show me. Show me the drawing room. At once.'

He ran to the door. Porlock, returning from giving instructions to the kitchen, was unceremoniously thrust aside.

Lord Ryde was hot on his heels, closely followed by Mr Martin, who, in his excitement, forgot to give way to Sir William, who in his turn, elbowed his way through the door, closely followed by Mrs Bascombe, Miss Fairburn, and Lady Elliott. Porlock, nearly bursting with curiosity, brought up the rear.

On reaching the drawing room, Mr Bascombe paused in the doorway for a moment, surveying the wreckage. The windows were shuttered, but enough light found its way through the chinks to show a disordered room full of shattered chairs and discarded fire irons. Lady Elliott modestly averted her eyes from the blood-stained fire tongs.

Presiding over the chaos, the disapproving portrait of old Lord Ryde hung wildly askew.

For one moment, everyone surveyed the mess in silence. Elinor held her breath, convinced that something important was about to happen.

And it did.

Mr George Bascombe began to laugh. He sagged against the doorpost and laughed. He leaned forwards, put his hands on his knees, and gasped for breath. For a moment, Mrs Bascombe wondered whether his fever had returned.

'George? Georgie? Are you ill again? Why are you laughing?

'Because it's funny, Elinor. It's so dammed funny. All those wasted years. For everyone. Well, not for me, of course. For me it was the best thing that could ever have happened. But no, it's not funny really. It's a tragedy that should never have happened. And he moved the portrait which is the funniest thing of all. I shouldn't be laughing. I'm sorry.'

He leaned his head back against the door and visibly

struggled to regain his composure. Even with his best effort, his voice still trembled as he said, 'May I see the library, please, Lord Ryde?'

Lord Ryde, who had been standing very still and very silent, curtly indicated that Mr Bascombe should precede him. Porlock, sensing A Dramatic Moment, threw open the doors with a flourish to disclose nothing more exciting than Margaret, carefully laying out the cups and saucers. Her face gave nothing away, but her heart was beating with excitement – and some exertion too, for as with Porlock and Munch, she, Janet, and Eliza, and even Mrs Munch herself, had been the protagonists in an extended and vigorous discussion over exactly whose duty it was to bring the fresh beverages to the library. Margaret, a sensible and pragmatic girl, had achieved victory by simply picking up the tray and marching out of the kitchen, leaving her lesser opponents in disarray behind her.

Her task completed, Margaret withdrew discreetly and hopefully to the corner of the room, only to catch Mr Porlock's eye. The message was clear. Margaret trailed disappointedly from the library.

Her intervention had served a useful purpose, however. Everyone seated themselves and a period of calm returned.

'So,' said Lord Ryde. 'Behold, the library. Almost exactly as you left it.'

George Bascombe turned slowly. 'Not quite. You moved the portrait.'

'What of it?'

'That's why they attacked the drawing room.'

'Because I moved the portrait?'

'Exactly.'

'Are you insane? It has no value. I can't even remember who painted it.'

Mr Bascombe could contain himself no longer; his excitement bubbled over and Lord Ryde was suddenly confronted by a younger version of George as he must once

179

have been.

'Not the portrait itself, sir, but what it concealed. And I'm afraid I do owe you an apology, Lord Ryde. A very large apology. Tell me, when Major Pirie and – I suppose I should refer to her as his sister – when they arrived, they were shown into the drawing room?'

'Yes,' said Elinor swiftly. 'They were.'

'And were they alone for any length of time?'

'Yes,' said Lord Ryde in his turn. 'They were.'

'Yes,' said Elinor, excited without knowing why. 'And do you remember, my lord, when we entered, they were examining the portrait of your father?'

George shook his head. 'Not the portrait, Elinor. They were trying to see what it concealed.'

'Dear God,' shrieked Lady Elliott, much to her husband's consternation. 'I shall go insane in a moment. For heaven's sake tell us – what does the portrait conceal?'

'Did.' said Mr Bascombe. 'What *did* the portrait conceal?'

Sir William prudently removed the fire irons from Lady Elliott's immediate vicinity.

George relented. 'I beg your pardon ma'am, I didn't mean to tease you.'

He reached up and with some difficulty removed the dismal landscape now adorning the space where the portrait had previously hung.

Everyone stared blankly at the blank panelling.

Mr Bascombe would not have been human if he had not prolonged the moment slightly. 'The portrait, Lady Elliot, concealed – this.'

With a flourish, he touched a spot on the mantle and creakily a portion of the panelling slid a few inches and then jerked to a halt.

Chapter Fourteen

For long seconds, nothing happened. No one moved. All eyes were riveted to the opening in the panelling.

Mr Bascombe pulled himself together. Dusting off his dirty fingers, he turned to Lord Ryde.

'Sir, I do owe you an apology. It never occurred to me that you were unaware of the true location of Lord Ryde's safe. Yes, he kept that big iron monstrosity for the look of the thing. He made sure the servants saw where their wages were kept and so on, but you know what he was like. Everything must be kept close. Only he must know the secret. So he kept his valuables in his second safe. Which no one but he knew existed.'

'Except you.'

Elinor could not look at Lord Ryde's face.

'He told you of this secret?'

'Yes, he did.'

'You knew?'

'I did, sir, yes.'

A long silence fell.

'And you told the Piries?'

'Indirectly, sir, I must have done. At some point in my fever, I must have mentioned the existence of this safe and they travelled here to try their luck. They must have been appalled when they saw the state of the – I mean, of course, that they were probably quite surprised that the estate did not show more signs of prosperity, but since they were here anyway ...' He shrugged. 'But, of course, you had moved the portrait and they broke into the wrong room.'

Sir William assisted Mrs Bascombe to a chair. 'I think we should all sit down again.'

Porlock, ears dropping off with excitement under his expressionless exterior began, as slowly as he could possibly manage it, to pour the tea.

Sir William continued. 'Let us piece together the events of That Night as best we can. Mr George Bascombe arrives at Ryde House and is shown into the library where old Lord Ryde is sitting at his desk. Lord Ryde furnishes him with clothing and a small sum of money for his travels. This he takes from what everyone in the world believes to be the safe in which he keeps his valuables. Mr Bascombe accepts with thanks and then departs. Mr Bascombe, what was Lord Ryde doing when you left?'

'He was finishing his letter, sir. As I looked back from the French windows, he was affixing his seal, and then he turned and placed it in his concealed safe. Then he nodded at me, wished me luck, and I left.'

'How did he look?'

'Ill, sir. Tired, very pale. And his hands were shaking.'

'Did he close this safe?' Sir William gestured at the partially opened panel.

'He did.'

'I think, my lord, that shortly after Mr Bascombe left, Lord Ryde suffered his stroke. I have heard that on many occasions, he struggled to speak or to make himself understood. Sadly, to no avail. This must have been the information he was endeavouring to convey.' Sir William looked across the room and drew a very deep breath. 'Since it appears no one was even aware of its existence, I think, sir, there is a very good chance that whatever was in there that night – is still there now.'

Mrs Bascombe caught her breath as the implications became clear.

Lord Ryde stood rooted in the middle of the room, facing the half-open panel. His face gave no clue to his emotions but Elinor could well guess some of the thoughts running through his head.

Sir William cleared his throat. 'I understand you may wish to inspect the possible contents in privacy, my lord, but accusations have been made and in the interests of fair play, it might be beneficial to both parties to have an independent witness present. My dear, I am sorry to ask you to vacate the only other habitable room in the building, but I'm sure you can appreciate the delicacy of the situation.'

Nothing in Lady Elliott's face revealed her intense disappointment at not being present for the climax to the extraordinary events of the last seven days. Sir William would have to suffer for this infamy in the privacy of his own home.

'Of course, Sir William.' She rose and shook out her skirt with every appearance of wifely submission. 'We shall return to the dining room.'

'No!'

The word might have been forced out of Lord Ryde. He continued grudgingly. 'No. We have all been involved in this – adventure.' He managed a smile. 'I would not deprive you of this moment, ma'am. Pray be seated.' Gathering himself with an effort, he said quietly, 'Charles, if you would be so good.'

Elinor, after one look at his face, clasped her hands tightly in her lap and struggled not to cry.

Mr Martin set his shoulder to the panel and Lord Ryde pulled. With the grating noise of dry wood on dry wood, the panel jerked open further, to reveal a dark interior. Porlock, ever ready to anticipate events, lighted a candelabrum and presented it to Mr Martin.

With Mr Martin lighting his way, Lord Ryde bent forward into the hole.

Elinor was sure her heartbeat must be clearly audible to everyone in the room.

The silence dragged on.

'Well,' demanded Sir William breathlessly. 'What can you see, man? Out with it!'

Lord Ryde turned from the concealed safe and with one swift movement, swept his desk clear. Pens, inkwells, papers, account books – all flew across the room.

Lady Elliot jumped violently in her seat and Mrs Bascombe, hardly realising what she did, slipped a cold hand into hers. She and Miss Fairchild exchanged glances. Even Mr Bascombe leaned forward in anticipation.

She heard Lord Ryde murmur something to Mr Martin who gave the candelabrum to Porlock and accepted an object from his lordship. The next moment, he placed a cashbox on the desk. Then another. And then another. That they were heavy could easily be seen by the effort he had to make.

A number of jewel boxes followed and were carefully placed alongside. Some ancient ledgers were stacked at one end of the desk and a crackling, brittle pile of yellow documents laid on top of them with some care.

There followed a long silence.

'Is that all of it?' enquired Sir William.

'Just this,' came the muffled reply, and Lord Ryde's head and shoulders somewhat dustily reappeared. He was holding a letter and the seal could clearly be seen.

Old Lord Ryde's last letter from which his son could not tear his eyes.

'Well, bless my soul,' said Sir William breathlessly. 'It's been here all along. None of it ever left the building and no one ever knew. Except for you, Mr Bascombe, and you weren't here.'

'Well, I'm here now,' said Georgie, somewhat defiantly.

Lord Ryde lifted his head and re-entered the world.

'You are indeed, Mr Bascombe, and I owe you an apology. An unreserved apology. I shall understand if you choose not to accept it, but whether you do or do not, rest assured I shall do everything in my power to scotch the rumours arising from your hasty departure. I really do not know what to say …'

'No need, no need,' said Mr Bascombe hastily, and indeed for one perilous moment, it seemed that strong emotion might rear its ugly head, but fortunately, Porlock coughed loudly and requested whether, in view of the occasion, Lord Ryde would permit him to serve wine to his guests.

Lord Ryde was graciously pleased to do so and his guests spent the next half hour examining the contents of the cash boxes and taking out the jewellery, which was, as Lord Ryde had once mentioned, very ugly indeed.

'But it can all be reset,' said Lady Elliot with a significant glance at Elinor, which did not go unnoticed by her husband. Elinor, however, was in a world of her own, watching Lord Ryde, who had not touched his wine but was still holding the letter.

Sir William rose to his feet.

'You look pale, Lady Elliott. Perhaps a turn outside in the sunshine will restore your colour.'

'No, I don't,' responded the wife of his bosom, before recollecting herself. 'Yes, actually, I believe I do feel extremely pale, now you come to mention it, my dear. These last twenty-four hours have been most trying. I am persuaded Miss Fairchild would benefit also.'

'Yes, indeed,' said Miss Fairburn, rising to her feet with alacrity. 'I think a little fresh air will be most beneficial.'

Mr Martin, torn between his duty to Lord Ryde and his inclination to accompany Miss Fairchild, uncharacteristically dithered.

'Yes, go, Charles,' said Lord Ryde, still without looking up from the letter. 'You may as well join the exodus in search of unpolluted ventilation.

'Well, if you are certain I can't be useful here, sir.'

'Later, perhaps, but not now, Charles, if you don't mind.'

The door closed behind them. Their voices could be heard crossing the hall until, eventually, they died away and only

Mrs Bascombe and Lord Ryde remained.

Elinor could not help reflecting that never before could such a large inheritance have been greeted by complete disinterest on one side and complete dismay on the other. Lord Ryde had eyes for nothing but his father's letter and she herself was coming to terms with the fact that there was now no reason for Lord Ryde to delay his departure for America. She had always known that he would go and now he had the wherewithal to pursue his goal. He could go now. This very moment. Or he could simply drive up to London at the earliest opportunity and resume his notorious ways. Or decamp for the continent and the attractions of its superior gaming houses. There was certainly nothing to keep him at Ryde House any longer.

On the other hand, there was nothing to keep her at Westfield now, either. George was home at last, bringing his own fortune with him. All her efforts, all her scrimping and saving, all those carefully planned schemes to confound their creditors – all was now as naught because George didn't need any of it.

She cast a glance at Lord Ryde, still staring at his unopened letter. She had a sudden vision of him sitting, unmoving, down through the long years, slowly growing as grey and dusty and hopeless as the rest of Ryde House. Something she would not be able to bear to watch.

She got up to go.

'Where are you going?' he said, sharply.

'In truth, I hardly know, my lord.'

'John.'

'John, then.'

Rousing himself, he noted with some amusement, but no surprise, that she paid no attention to the treasure laid out on the desk before him. Golden guineas, rolls of bank notes, fabulous jewels – it might none of it have existed for all the heed she gave.

'Is the letter addressed to you?'

'It is. Addressed to me in my father's own hand and sealed with his own seal.'

'Will you open it?'

'I'm almost afraid to. These were his last words in this world. Perhaps he felt his stroke coming on. What was so important he had to force himself to write? Suppose, Elinor, just suppose his last words to me are of anger and pain and blame. How shall I bear it?'

Eleanor regarded him carefully for a moment. 'Then give it to me.'

'What will you do with it?'

'Throw it in the fire, of course. If you do not wish to discover what was so important to him that he preferred to finish his letter rather than ring for assistance then I will destroy it now, my lord and you may take your new-found wealth and depart for America, leaving this house and its memories behind for ever.'

'And you, Elinor. Shall I leave you behind for ever?'

'You will not be granted the opportunity. I shall return to Westfield, pack a bag, and follow you every step of the way. Wherever you go. I have no knowledge of America or its people, but I expect I shall pick it all up very easily.'

'Yes,' said his lordship bitterly. 'And a fine fellow I shall look with everyone saying I seduced you –'

'Well, you did –'

'– and lured you away from the safety of your home. I can just see George Bascombe pursuing me across England and putting a bullet through me on some lonely heath somewhere while you look on and – why are you laughing?'

'Heaven knows. After all, it's not as if the return of George Bascombe or the sudden acquisition of fabulous wealth is anything to laugh about. I suspect my intellect is disordered. You do very well to abandon me, my lord, before I become totally deranged.'

'Shameless is a more apt description of you, Mrs Bascombe.'

'Elinor.'

'Elinor, then.'

He looked down again. 'What shall I do, Elinor?'

'Open it. It is always better to know, don't you think?

With fingers that were not quite steady, he broke open the seal and carefully unfolded the crackling paper. He stared sightlessly for a few minutes and then passed it over.

'Read it to me, Elinor, if you would, please.'

Taking it from him, she cleared her throat and read slowly.

My dear John,

For some time now, it has been in my mind to write to you, and something has occurred tonight which makes it vital I write without delay.

There has been a series of unfortunate events at Westfield, culminating in young George Bascombe being forced to flee his home with nothing but the clothes on his back. I have done what I can for him and will continue to do so in the future, but his distress and despair have brought home to me, as nothing else could, the folly of my own actions all those years ago. As Ned Bascombe has done to young George, so did I do to you, my own son. I could have stood by you as you recovered from your wound and I did not. I could have recalled you when it became apparent that Lady Reeth did not take her marriage vows quite as seriously as she should, and I did not. I could at any time have extended the hand of fatherly love to you. I did none of those things.

We were both at fault, John, but mine is the blame. As the possessor of a supposedly older and wiser head, I should long ago have made the first move to bridge the gaping chasm that has arisen between us. I do so now.

With you in mind, I have recently purchased the manor of Fernleigh, some twenty miles to the north. It is small and run down, but I think with clever management and some hard work it could be made to show a profit in a very short time. I intend to sign it over to you for you to manage yourself and look forward to seeing what sort of job you make of setting it back on its feet again. I shall not interfere – unless asked to do so, of course – and I must admit, I find the thought of you and I, two respectable landowners discussing the finer points of crop rotation and animal husbandry over a glass of wine, curiously amusing.

I shall send copies of this letter to every embassy throughout Europe in the hope, the desperate hope, that one day it will find you, wherever you happen to be.

Come home soon, Johnnie, I miss you.

Your loving father.

Very, very carefully, Elinor laid the letter down on the desk. Without withdrawing his gaze from the fire, Lord Ryde placed his hand protectively over it. The silence in the room grew very loud.

She had found herself almost unbearably moved by this simple, heartfelt plea from the father and could only guess at the effect it must have had on his son.

Rising to her feet, she crossed to Lord Ryde's chair to stand next to him. He neither moved nor spoke. Elinor could guess at the thoughts running through his head. The wasted years. The missed opportunities. The series of mistakes, bad luck, and unfortunate coincidences that had brought him now, to this time, this place, and the sudden dreadful revelation that a large part of his life could have been very different.

Different, yes, but not necessarily better.

How would they have fared together, these two obstinate, stiff-necked men? For how long would they have been able to endure each other's company before the proud, controlling

189

parent clashed with the wilful, independent son? Now, of course, they would never know.

She surfaced to find Lord Ryde watching her.

'What is it, Elinor?'

'I was just thinking,' she said softly, 'that the missed opportunities, for which you are blaming yourself, might not be too great a cause for regret.'

'You could be right,' he said. 'A year – perhaps two, before we started to rub against each other again. Or even worse, I might have married some local girl and be the besieged parent of any number of ghastly offspring.'

'A fate worse than death indeed,' she agreed quietly.

He leaned against her and she gently touched his hair. He remembered the warmth and softness of her, but even though he was sure they would not be disturbed, he could not reach for her as he once done in this very room.

'So, my lord …'

'John.'

'John. What now?'

'What do you mean – what now?'

'Well, what are your plans? Will you take your wealth and proceed to America as planned, to embark upon your new life?'

'I don't have to go as far as America for a new life.'

'True,' she agreed. 'London has many attractions, to many of which you will be able to succumb with all speed.'

He barked a short laugh. 'And find myself prey to every matchmaking mama in town? I can tell you now, Mrs Bascombe – '

'Elinor.'

'Elinor – once word of my wealth gets out, I won't be able to move for the vast hordes of people who always thought my father to have been harsh and over-hasty, or who knew all along there must have been some terrible mistake. George Bascombe will find exactly the same thing. If only the world possessed as much compassion as it does

190

hindsight ...'

He trailed away, lost in thought and Elinor watched him anxiously.

'And what of you, Elinor? Today has been a day of revelation for you, too.'

'It has indeed. I think, when the shock has subsided a little, today will have been a happy day.'

'For you, perhaps. You will return to Westfield with Mr Bascombe, not to pick up the reins of your old, restricted life, but suddenly to enjoy luxury and much deserved extravagance. You will have that visit to Bath, Elinor. You will travel, see new sights, meet new people. Your life will change beyond all recognition.'

'Yes,' said Elinor, dismally.

His lordship did not appear to notice.

'You will have fine clothes, more servants, and best of all, financial security at last.'

'Yes,' said Elinor, drearily.

'All the unremitting toil of these last years when you worked so hard to pull the estate back together, all your careful schemes for the future, all that is done with. You can hand the management of Westfield to Mr Bascombe and be free at last.'

'Well, you needn't sound so cheerful about it,' said Mrs Bascombe with some asperity. 'Long days of pointless embroidery and trying new ways of wearing my hair are not my idea of happiness.'

'I am very pleased to hear you say that, because I have a proposition to put to you, Mrs Bascombe.'

'Elinor.'

'Elinor. It seems to me that you are an excellent estate manager without an estate to manage and I have an estate crying out for an excellent estate manager. What do you say, Mrs Bascombe? Can I make you an offer of –?'

Elinor groped for words. 'Are you – I cannot believe – how could you – are you offering me employment?'

'What? No, of course not. What on earth made you think that? How could I, with any propriety, offer a female the job of my estate manager? Where on earth did you get that idea from?'

'Oh, I don't know, possibly from your less-than-romantic speech about estate management, perhaps.'

'Elinor, you have been itching to get your hands on my neglected acres from the moment we first met. You've already made a start on my dilapidated house. To say nothing of my deplorable self.'

'What?'

'And now I offer it all to you.'

'I can't work for you, my lord. George would never allow such a thing. Obviously I would be happy to give you my advice should you care to consult me, but …'

'Elinor, will you please rid yourself of this ridiculous idea you have of working for me. I'm asking you to marry me.'

'So I am to marry you in order to dust your furniture, repair your land, and protect you from matchmaking mothers?'

He took her hands and held them to his chest.

'No, Elinor, you are to marry me because I adore you and am now utterly convinced I cannot live without you. You have galloped into my life, opening up my heart and my house, and bringing light and life into both. I find the thought of going even one day without hearing your voice or seeing your face quite unbelievably painful. You must marry me, Elinor, because I love you to distraction and beyond.'

Mrs Bascombe retreated around the desk on legs that suddenly felt unable to support her.

To gain time, she said slowly, 'You are asking me to marry you?'

'Yes, Mrs Bascombe.'

'Elinor.'

Slowly, he rose to his feet and walked around the desk.

'Elinor, I hope very much that you will do me the honour

192

_'

'Why would you want to marry me?'

'Well, as previously mentioned – run-down house, neglected estate, oh and there are the Munches to manage, of course …'

'How is that any sort of incentive?' said Mrs Bascombe, drawing herself up and doing her best to ignore both his lordship's proximity and her own wildly beating heart.

'Well, how about the Ryde diamonds,' suggested his lordship, pulling over a number of jewel boxes.

'They're hideous.'

'I really think you should consider their value before you reject them out of hand.'

'Nothing in the world could compel me to wear the Ryde diamonds –' began Elinor.

His lordship's shoulders slumped dramatically.

'– in their present setting. I'm afraid, my lord, said Elinor, virtuously, 'that nothing you can say would enable me to look more favourably on your suit.'

'Well, there's the title, of course.'

'Oh yes,' said Elinor, apparently much struck by this. 'I had forgotten the title.'

'You would be Lady Ryde.'

'I might be, yes.'

He moved quickly, pulled her to him, and held her close.

'You would be my lady,' he said thickly into her hair. 'And I could shower you with reset diamonds in the moonlight.'

His lady caught her breath and decided it was her duty to take every advantage of this probably very fleeting moment of generosity.

Stroking his cheek, she whispered, 'I would so much rather have a herd of shorthorns, my lord.'

'If that is what it takes,' said Lord Ryde, adjusting his ideas somewhat, 'then I shall shower you with shorthorns instead. Although God knows how. I expect Charles will think of a way. He's very ingenious.'

'In that case, my lord, I do not hesitate to accept your flattering and hopefully shorthorn-filled proposal of marriage.'

'I thought you might,' he whispered, his breath warm in her ear.

Mrs Bascombe, skilled negotiator, was not so easily won over.

'I shall want to see the herd first before finally committing myself, you understand.'

'You shall inspect each one personally,' promised his lordship, running his fingers down her slim neck and being rewarded with a sharp intake of breath. She melted against him and for some time, all thoughts of livestock and anything else were driven from both their minds.

'So,' said Mrs Bascombe, some minutes later, attempting unsuccessfully to straighten his lordship's disordered cravat, 'really, there is no need for me to return to Westfield, is there?'

His lordship put her from him.

'Indeed there is, Mrs Bascombe and I declare I am shocked at this lapse of propriety in the future Lady Ryde. You will return to Westfield with Mr Bascombe, whither I will visit in seven days' time, formally to request your hand in marriage. It is to be hoped he gives his consent because, although I've never tried it, I have heard that elopements can be dashed tricky affairs Especially if one's bride insists on encumbering herself with an entourage of butlers, maids, shorthorns, over-spirited chestnuts, and Lord knows what. Why, at that rate it would take me a month to get you all to Gretna.'

Mrs Bascombe snuggled against his chest. 'I have no doubt you would manage it splendidly.'

'Well, yes, I would,' said his lordship modestly, 'but that would be because I would be concentrating on you in the moonlight and leave everything else to Charles.'

'Hm,' said Mrs Bascombe, thoughtfully. 'Perhaps I should marry Mr Martin instead.'

'You could certainly try,' said his lordship unflatteringly, 'but I doubt he even sees you if Miss Fairchild is in the vicinity. Which reminds me …' he released Mrs Bascombe as he spoke and began to rummage around the documents on his desk.

Beyond remarking how quickly the romance had faded, Mrs Bascombe made no complaint, merely waiting quietly until a small packet of documents headed Fernleigh Manor in the parish of Whittington was presented for her inspection.

'For Charles,' announced his lordship. 'On the occasion of his marriage. I myself expect to spend what little remains of my life as a victim of oppression and abuse, but there's no reason why Charles and Miss Fairchild shouldn't live happily ever after.'

Mrs Bascombe could not have said why she chose that moment to burst into tears.

His lordship regarded her in some dismay.

'Tears? So soon? Should I buy you one of the new seed drills? Would that help?'

She dried her tears and nodded vigorously. 'Oh yes, that would be delightful. And if we set some men to clearing your three fields bordering mine, we could have them manured and sown for a winter crop in no time.'

'I am a lost man,' he sighed. 'I have fallen into the hands of a harpy who will stop at nothing to ensure my future happiness and prosperity. How shall I bear it?'

'Courage, my lord. Given your self-admitted advanced age and decrepitude, the chances are that you will not live long enough to suffer greatly.'

'True.' He brightened. 'Shall we rejoin the others, Elinor and offer them the opportunity to rejoice in my abbreviated life expectancy?'

'In a minute,' she whispered, and reached for him again …

If you enjoyed *A Bachelor Establishment*,
why not try Jodi Taylor's bestselling
Chronicles of St Mary's series . . .

'So tell me, Dr Maxwell, if the whole of History lay before you . . . where would you go? What would you like to witness?'

When Madeleine Maxwell is recruited by the St Mary's Institute of Historical Research, she discovers the historians there don't just study the past – they revisit it.

But one wrong move and History will fight back – to the death. And she soon discovers it's not just History she's fighting . . .

HEADLINE

A Symphony of Echoes

Wherever the historians go, chaos is sure to follow . . .

Dispatched to Victorian London to seek out Jack
the Ripper, things go badly wrong when he finds the
St Mary's historians first. Stalked through the
fog-shrouded streets of Whitechapel, Max is soon
running for her life. Again.

And that's just the start. Max finds herself in
a race against time when an old enemy is intent on
destroying St Mary's. An enemy willing, if necessary,
to destroy History itself . . .

HEADLINE

A SECOND CHANCE

I could have been a bomb-disposal expert, or a volunteer for the Mars mission, or a firefighter, something safe and sensible. But, no, I had to be an historian.

It began well. A successful assignment to 17th-century Cambridge to meet Isaac Newton, and another to witness the historic events at The Gates of Grief. So far so good.

But then came the long-awaited jump to the Trojan War that changed everything. And for Max, nothing will ever be the same again.

With the bloody Battle of Agincourt playing out around her, Max risks everything on one last desperate gamble to save a life and learns the true meaning of a second chance.

HEADLINE

Sometimes, surviving is all you have left.

Max and Leon are safe at last. Or so they think.

Snatched from her own world and dumped into a new one,
Max is soon running for her life. Again.

From a 17th-century Frost Fair to Ancient Egypt; from
Pompeii to 8th-century Scandinavia; Max and Leon are
pursued up and down the timeline, playing a dangerous
game of hide-and-seek, until finally they're forced to take
refuge at St Mary's where a new danger awaits them.

Max's happily ever after
is going to have to wait a while . . .

HEADLINE

NO TIME LIKE THE PAST

A fete worse than death.

The St Mary's Institute of Historical Research has finally recovered from its wounds and it's business as usual for those rascals in the History Department.

From being trapped in the Great Fire of London to an unfortunately timed comfort break at Thermopylae, which leaves the fate of the western world hanging in the balance, Max must struggle to get History back on track.

But first, they must get through the St Mary's Fete – which is sure to end badly for everyone.

Only one thing is certain, life at St Mary's is never dull.

HEADLINE

HISTORY WILL NEVER BE THE SAME AGAIN...

BOOK ONE

BOOK TWO

BOOK THREE

BOOK FOUR

BOOK FIVE

BOOK SIX

BOOK SEVEN

BOOK EIGHT

BOOK NINE

BOOK TEN

SHORT STORIES

THE CHRONICLES OF ST MARY'S